# In Conversations with Strangers

Brenda Cheers

BIRDCALL PUBLISHING AUSTRALIA

brendacheersbooks.com

First Edition

Cover image © Wisky | iStockphoto
Andrew's image © Olga Vasilkova | Dreamstime.com
Marge's image © Alevtina Guzova | Dreamstime.com
Anne's image © Gongqi Zhang (aka Michael Zhang) | Dreamstime.com
Jenny's image © Dan (Danjo) Williams
Author image Sargaison – Brisbane Headshots
Page 138 Excerpt from *We of the Never Never* by Jeannie Gunn, first published in 1905

ISBN-13: 978-0-9922907-2-6

*To those people who give me the time and space to write –*
*I thank you with all my heart.*

Also by Brenda Cheers

*In a House in Yemen*

*In Times of Trouble*

*In Strange Worlds*

# In Conversations with Strangers

# CHAPTER ONE

When I look back on that terrible day in Brisbane, I wonder how sane I was as I drove out of my driveway. How did I look? Were my teeth bared and was my hair standing on end? Or did I look like a hurt and frightened child? In fact, I was a woman who had just witnessed something so shocking that I could only live on my instincts, and they told me to get as far from that place as quickly as possible.

I remember fumbling with the keys, cursing when they dropped to the floor of the car. I remember trying to push the key into the ignition with shaking hands. I remember the engine coming to life, still warm from when I drove into the garage only a short time before. My foot slammed down on the accelerator, and the SUV shot out of the garage and onto the driveway.

By the time I reached the street I was already driving fast. A small dog appeared at my right front wheel, and I stamped on the brake pedal. The dog's owner yanked fiercely on its leash and began mouthing abuse. I ignored him, and my foot found the accelerator again.

I swerved right onto Union Street, finding some comfort in the whine of the over-revved engine. At the end of the street I turned right again without thought or caution. I was vaguely aware that a white car had to brake hard and swerve to avoid me. I just kept accelerating and sped down Miskin Street.

I heard a siren coming from behind. The rear vision mirror was filled with flashing blue and red lights. I pulled over.

Watching the officer walk toward me, I felt an odd detachment, like I wasn't present in my body. I closed my eyes and took some deep breaths.

"Can I see your Driver's Licence please, Miss?" He was holding out his hand.

I looked around for my handbag. Had I left it on the table at home? No, I didn't think so. I swivelled around to look in the back. There it was. I rummaged for my purse and extracted the licence.

"You didn't stop at the sign back there and I almost hit you. Then I had a hard time catching up." He looked at me for a long few seconds, and his voice softened. "Your licence says you live in Union Street. Is everything alright?"

His voice was that of a middle-aged man. He was being kind and I hated that. I just needed to be driving, getting as far away from that place as I could. I mumbled something about being fine.

"Have you been drinking?"

I shook my head.

"Look, I'm not going to book you this time, but you could have injured yourself or someone else badly back there. Just slow down and be careful, eh?"

I nodded without looking at him. He sighed and handed the licence back. I murmured my thanks, indicated carefully and then pulled back onto the street. As soon as the police car was out of sight, I stamped on the accelerator again.

I continued in this way for some time, but the roads in the Western Suburbs of Brisbane are not designed for high speed escape. There were traffic lights and pedestrians and a great many pushbike riders. I just became more and more frustrated and angry. Where was I going anyway? I had no idea.

A sudden impulse had me making a squealing U-turn, and I began heading west. I reached for the GPS and entered a destination. I felt a small lift in spirits. I had an idea of where to head, and once I got there I would decide where to go after that. At least I had a plan of sorts. I would be in Roma by nightfall.

I fumbled in my handbag again for my sunglasses, settled back in the seat, and let the calming voice of the GPS guide me away from the hell that Brisbane had just become.

What I remember most about that first day of travelling was how I fluctuated between practical and highly emotional. I could plan what to do in the next few days with clarity and good intuition, but then crash down to helplessness. I am not a person given to strong emotion, and the state I was in was rare and bewildering.

The planning helped. I started writing a list in my head, visualising it as if I had written it with pen and paper. I could see the lines and feel my favourite pen between my fingers as the words formed. It was a welcome distraction.

At one stage I began thinking about money, trying to work out exactly how much I had in the various accounts and term deposits. Then I could see a picture of the banking website, my accounts lined up neatly with the sum of $75,396 at the bottom. I could make that last a long time.

I slowed at a known speed camera site. Fines would always be sent to work - one drawback of a company car - and the Boss would always hand them to me with raised eyebrows and downturned mouth. I had worked for him for many years and always tried to do the right thing. Speeding, however, was just something I seemed powerless to control, and I was always scrambling to save myself from a loss of licence.

The car... my work. I'd have to call the Boss and tell him that I needed some emergency leave, and also that I needed the car. I pictured him sitting at his desk, a look of puzzlement on his face. I couldn't talk to him now. I'd wait until I could speak calmly, however long that took. I pictured my desk, vacant but tidy. My work was up to date. The Boss was at golf. I had until early Monday morning to explain myself.

Thinking of work made me form another picture in my mind. I saw Chris striding across the used car lot. I heard myself wailing before I realised I was doing it. I began thumping the steering wheel with both hands, accidentally activating the horn. The white lines were not straight, but dancing before me, writhing and curling in front of the car. Thinking back now, I wonder how I appeared to other drivers. In my grief I didn't consider it, but now I realise how dangerous I must have looked. Eventually I began breathing deeply, calming myself.

West of Toowoomba it feels like you are driving on top of the world, and, with the skies suddenly clear of cloud, I certainly had that sensation. There is a sense of freedom about driving 'out West', and because both driving and travelling alone are my favourite things to do, I began to feel a sense of joy in strange juxtaposition to my grief and anger.

After two more hours the shadows began to lengthen, and a glow infused the sky. I pulled over to the side of the road and climbed stiffly from the car, breathing in the clean air as I did so. The atmosphere had that special quality where noises travelled differently, and I heard distant birds, their cries echoing across the plains.

There was something missing however—something that could have made the scene perfect. I searched the sky and then realised what day it was. A no-moon day. The moon would not appear at any stage or in any form. That's why I had driven home. I wanted to take advantage of the magical lovemaking properties of this special day.

No-moon days have dark magic in them too, though. They are known for communication problems, tactical errors, untimely deaths, suicides and, of course, shattered hearts.

In my early teens it became trendy to be interested in astrology. My best friend and I went to the school library after the final bell had sounded for the day and researched our star signs and what it all meant in our lives. I discovered that, as a Cancerian, my ruling planet was the Moon. The Moon? I'd been cheated! Everybody knew the Moon wasn't a planet! I was devastated.

It wasn't a bad thing, however. Further research showed that Cancerians were fortunate to have such a strong and steady presence in their skies. It was always there, except for those no-moon days. Other astrological houses saw their ruling planets infrequently, and often these visits caused trials and mayhem. Mine was with me always, or nearly so.

The years went by, and I hadn't given the subject much further thought. That was until a conversation with a co-worker.

I was walking out to a car and a manager was following me, wanting to wish me a happy birthday. "So you're a Cancerian, eh? Just like my wife."

"That's right," I said, trying to remember her.

"Are you affected by the moon too? I can tell when it's full just by looking at her."

"No, I don't think I am. What happens?"

"She gets….I dunno… really energetic and creative. She shines. It's bloody wonderful."

I stood, deep in thought, trying to figure out if it applied to me.

"But then it goes away and she with it. That's bloody awful."

This new information hummed away in my brain all day. As soon as I got home I decided to put it to the test.

I have always kept a diary. That night I looked back through the entries for the current year, noting the events around the full moon. I became excited and reached up to the top of my wardrobe to find the two previous volumes. Yes, there was a definite trend happening. In the days leading up to the full moon, and for a day or so afterwards, life was energetic and interesting. If something weird or strange happened, it was often around the time of a new moon. How could this be used to my advantage?

From then on, whenever I had a major event to organise, I would check the calendar and make sure it was scheduled for when the moon was full, or as close to it as I could get. If there was something I needed to do that required more energy than usual, I'd delay it until that time. It worked very, very well.

I guess I've become fairly obsessive about it since then. I conserve energy around the times of new moons. I'm more careful in what I say to people. I watch the negative forces.

I can tell you many more things. I had a miscarriage on a moonless night. Several years later I gave birth on the day before a full moon. I took my son to the window the day after his birth and pointed to my lunar friend. "Look at the full moon, my lovely boy. You've been born at just the right time. You must be blessed."

The motel room in Roma was small but clean. An air conditioner hummed in the corner, and a bedside lamp was casting a soft light across the bed. I had a tiredness of body and spirit that was weighing me down, and my first act in this strange room was to fall on the bed and into oblivion.

I woke hours later with a sense of disorientation that took me several moments to overcome. For that short time I was blissfully unaware of the events of the day, but when the brain retrieved the information, the horror of it hit with full force. I began sobbing.

After half an hour or so, I got impatient with myself and decided on some action. First I splashed cold water on my face and then I found a pen and a piece of paper. I'm not a person who can just make plans up as I go—definitely not a fly-by-the-seat-of-your-pants type. I need plans; I need to know where I'm headed and when I'll get there. Then I need to know where I'm going after that.

I cursed the fact I didn't have a map and now reception was closed. How could I plan my trip? Then I realised that my laptop was in the car. So was the broadband dongle. I almost broke into a run as I went out to retrieve them, feeling blessed that I had decided to take the laptop home earlier that day.

I was afraid the broadband dongle wouldn't have access to the satellite that far west, but it had excellent strength and soon I was looking at a map of the Matilda Highway. My car was an SUV, but not a rugged 4WD. I would need to stay on either sealed roads or dirt roads in good condition. At least it was the right time of year with the heavy rainfalls gone.

I decided not to stay on the Matilda Highway to the end, but to veer off to Darwin. Where to from there? I saw a place name that made me smile.

Broome. I had always wanted to go there, mainly to

see a phenomenon called "Staircase to the Moon". Occurring only between March and October, it is caused by the full moon rising over the mudflats of Roebuck Bay during low tide.

With that decision made I found new energy for preparations. I needed an excellent camera, tripod, and other accessories. I needed clothing and toiletries. I needed emergency supplies in case of the SUV breaking down. The list grew. Then I started another. By midnight I had three lists divided into categories and my trip planned down to the last detail.

I looked longingly at the mini bar. I really, really wanted to get drunk. I shook my head and looked away. That was something I definitely could not do. "Keep yourself good," I said aloud.

I was alone again. Alone was good. How many times had I fought for my freedom, for the right to live alone? I had two divorces behind me, caused mostly by the need to live by myself. I had felt suffocated through the later stages of the first marriage and ended it suddenly and without a backward glance. I had been feeling the same about the second one and was considering ending that too, just so I could be alone. That was until Chris came along, and everything changed.

# CHAPTER TWO

I had been away from work for a few days; there was a conference in Sydney after which I took some annual leave. After arriving at work early, I spent several solid hours catching up and then went to take some documents to the new car showroom. I found the kitchen quiet, so decided to make a coffee there.

I stood at the window and took deep sips from the cup. A group of people walked past and stopped just within my sight. My cup didn't make it to my lips again. I had forgotten it was there.

She was stunning. Tall and well-proportioned with cropped blonde hair and blue eyes, but it was her mouth that mesmerised. It was full and wide. When she laughed it took over her face. The three men, all salesmen, were crowding around her, acting like courtiers to a queen.

I became aware of someone standing behind me, also

watching. "That's the new salesperson, Christine Laws. Gorgeous, isn't she?"

I looked around to see Beth from reception, staring at Christine in admiration. I just nodded.

"The boys have been acting like bloody idiots since she started here last week. She seems oblivious."

"What's her story?"

"I don't know. I can't get to talk to her for all the men hanging around."

The group moved off, walking crookedly and laughing. It felt like the sun had disappeared behind a cloud.

I went back to the administration block, but found I couldn't focus on the pile of work on my desk. At twelve-thirty I took my lunch from my drawer and went back to the showroom kitchen. It was a place I normally avoided because at that time of the day it was chaotic. Salespeople don't get to sit down and eat like the rest of us. It's all high energy, with sales calls to be taken after one mouthful, or a customer in the showroom needing attention. Half-eaten meals lie scattered over the benches.

On that day I sat and started eating my sandwich. There was only one other person there and he was a used car salesperson, one I didn't know very well. He tried to start a conversation twice, but I withdrew as I often do, and we ate in silence.

The door burst open, and it seemed that hordes of people entered at once. Chris was at the head of the pack, balancing parcels wrapped in white paper. She got to the table and let them all fall. "Here's the cod for Shane," she said, handing a parcel to one of the boys. "The whiting, two of." Hands grasped at the packages. "The rest are plain chips."

She sat down and opened her own lunch, which turned out to be steamed fish and salad. The room was full of the sounds of ripping paper and conversations made with full-to-overflowing mouths. The smell of the fish and chips became nauseating. I packed up my lunch, stood, and left.

"Hey!" I could hear someone running up behind me.

I turned.

She was smiling with less certainty than before. "Hey, I'm Christine Laws. I'm sorry if we chased you out of there."

"Hi. I'm Janine. It's okay. Don't be sorry."

"Where do you work?"

"In Admin. I should have been eating over in that kitchen anyway."

"Ah, okay." She didn't move away but kept looking at

me. I realised I should say something.

"I hear you're a new salesperson."

"Yeah, just started last week. It's a fun place. I like it."

There was another pause. I couldn't think of a single thing to say, but then something came to mind.

"Have you joined the Social Club yet?"

"That was one of the first things I did."

"Great. There's a raffle going on at the moment. I'm selling the tickets if you're interested."

"What's the prize?"

"A weekend on the Gold Coast at that six-star hotel. All expenses paid."

"Wow, yeah. I'll walk over with you and buy some."

As we walked through the office, I saw everyone looking up at her. She was just like that.

"They're five dollars each, or ten for fifty dollars," I said. Chris frowned. "Sorry, a bad joke I know."

Then she got it. "Ha! Very funny. Hey, I really want to go and stay there so I'll buy eight. That'll just about clean me out."

"Who would you take if you won?"

"Hmmm... I don't know. Perhaps I'd take you for selling them to me. Who would you take?"

"Not my husband, that's for sure. Perhaps we could

make a deal. If I win, I take you. If you win, you take me."

"Yes! Great idea. We'd have a ball." She looked at her watch. "Oops, I'd better get back. I've got a test drive in a few minutes. Thanks honey-bunch."

"You're welcome. Good luck."


"Hey, Janine."

I looked up to see her standing at my desk.

"Christine! Hello."

"Busy?"

"A bit, but I'd kill for a coffee. I'll shout you one."

We took our cups out on to the smoking deck. It had a good view of the two dealerships. There was a lot of activity that morning, with cars being unloaded from long freighters and the used car salesmen re-arranging the lot.

Christine took a big sip of coffee. "It's a shame neither of us won the raffle. It would have been great."

"Yeah, I think it'll be wasted on Bob. What's he going to do in a place like that?"

We both laughed.

"I'm surprised he didn't ask you along."

She hooted. "He did! *As if!*"

That was the thing about Chris. She always made me

laugh and forget myself. I found I wasn't self-conscious or shy at all.

"Hey," she said. "There are drinks after work on Friday. Why don't we go together?"

The 'no' almost escaped my lips automatically, but then I thought about it. Why not? I could avoid David for a few hours at least. The moon would be close to full and I'd have lots of energy.

"Yes! I'd love that. Where is it being held?"

"Just up the road somewhere. I was told 'the usual place'. People forget I haven't been here long and don't know these things.

I'd seen the bills come through so was able to tell her the name of it.

"That's set then? We'll have fun. Gotta go. I'll see you later."

She downed the last of the coffee and waved goodbye.

I sat on the deck until she came into view downstairs, striding confidently across the car lot, waving and talking to people as she went. I am always in awe of people who move confidently through the world, and she was a master of it.


I rolled over on the sofa and groaned. It wasn't at all

comfortable and there was a streetlight shining through the curtains. How had I gotten myself into this?

The night had been fun. Chris saw me arrive and broke off her conversation to come over to greet me. She kissed me on both cheeks, European style, then took my hand and led me back to where she'd been standing. The Boss was there and did a double-take when he saw me. "Well, well...nice to see you at one of these, Janine."

I smiled and listened in on the conversation surrounding Chris. I didn't feel the need to join in; it was good just to listen to how she handled the various topics. I knew I could learn a lot from her about socialising. Late in the evening I became engrossed in a conversation with another of the administration staff. They were having trouble with their new smartphone and I was able to help them in many ways.

Soon I noticed the crowd had begun to dwindle. It was time to go home. I was looking for Chris to say goodbye when I realised she was right behind me. "Come back to my place for a while, okay? I'm not tired yet."

I looked at my watch. David would be wondering where I was. "No, I'd better go home. Thanks all the same."

"Aw, come on. I need some company. I won't keep you much longer."

Her flat was within walking distance, and the moon followed us as we walked lightly along the footpaths. The world had that glorious silvery sheen that only happens on those clear, still, full-mooned nights. Chris spoke all the way, commenting on the various personalities of the people we both worked with. I marvelled at her insight— how she could see past the facades that co-workers displayed. She could see their motives clearly. When I spoke to people I could only hear the words they were telling me, not the subtext. I took them literally. Very, very literally.

As she fiddled with the key in the door, she said, "Ignore the mess. I'm only renting this place short-term so haven't really unpacked much." I stepped through the door and felt a bit sick. Mess and confusion does that to me. Boxes were strewn over all the available floor space. Most had been opened and their contents had erupted. I forced a smile.

"What are we drinking then? I've got wine, whiskey, and vodka."

"Do you have any juice or mineral water? I'll have to drive home." I realised I had left my car back at the venue we'd just left.

"Don't be silly. You can crash here tonight. You can sleep on the sofa. I'll lend you some pyjamas."

She rummaged around in the refrigerator and produced some cheese. "Wine, I think. Okay?"

I was tackling so many issues at that moment that I couldn't think of a reply. I don't like 'crashing' anywhere. I don't like wearing other people's clothes. I wanted to be home, removing my makeup with my special cleanser and preparing to climb into my bed, which had crisp, clean, luxury weave 100 percent cotton sheets. I felt the wine glass being pushed into my hand, and then saw she had the cheese and crackers in one hand and her wine in the other and was leading the way to the lounge. She docked her mobile into a player and soon some smooth jazz filled the room. That calmed me a bit.

She started telling me why she'd left her job in Sydney and moved to Brisbane. It was to do with a man she was seeing, a co-worker who was married. It had been going on for a long time, but it all 'blew-up" and she thought it best to move away and make a fresh start. "He ended up being a bit of a bastard, really. In the panic to save his marriage he hung me out to dry."

I felt my eyes starting to close. "Oh, I've kept you up too long!" She rushed away and came back with a long, white t-shirt. "The most comfortable nightie in the world. The bathroom is through there. I'll let you go first."

That had been hours before. The sofa was definitely not made for sleeping. I tossed and turned again. My watch said two-fifteen.

I heard her voice coming from another room. "Can't sleep? I guess you're not very comfortable. I can hear you moving around from here. Come into my bed, it's huge."

So I rose from the sofa, and the moon watched silently as I padded softly into her bedroom. I entered her bed, and from that time onwards never really left it again. Oh, I went home to my husband and son, and acted like nothing had changed. They were used to my carefully arranged exterior and had no idea that, in Chris, I had just found the missing piece to my life.

Chris was quite simply everything I wasn't and I was everything she wasn't. This could have been good or it could have been disastrous. In fact, it was quite beautiful.

She was the Capricorn to my Cancer, making us the most compatible combination possible, astrologically speaking. She knew my traits and loved me for them, never being critical or frustrated by them. We made a striking couple: her tall blondeness to my short darkness; her fair complexion and blue eyes to my olive skin and brown eyes;

her plump roundness with full breasts to my androgynous body with a size B cup. Once we were in each other's arms nothing could pry us apart. Not for a long time, anyway.

After that first night in her bed, when it was nearly time for me to tear myself from her, she sat up and looked at me closely.

"I just realised what it is....who you remind me of!"

"Oh?"

"My Aunt Lily! She's my mother's sister. I've always loved her - such an unconventional person."

"I don't see myself as unconventional at all."

"Oh, I think you might be, behind that emotionless facade. I'm going to tell you Aunt Lily's qualities and if they relate to you, just nod. Okay?"

"Okay."

"Oh, and none of these qualities are negatives. They're just my Aunt Lily."

"Okay."

"A bit awkward socially, but gets by."

I nodded.

"Spatially challenged. No sense of direction. Bad at learning dance moves by watching someone else do it."

I laughed and nodded.

"If someone starts to talk to her about something she's

interested in she suddenly comes to life and dumps a whole lot of information on that person."

I thought about the smartphone advice I gave the night before. I nodded.

"She has a strong artistic side. She paints. Do you do anything artistic?"

"I write fiction."

"That's it then! She only wears natural fibres and comfortable clothes."

"True."

"Perfume smells too strong and she can't wear it."

"Yes."

"She prefers to live alone, but if she finds the right significant other can share her life with them."

I nodded.

"She is brilliant with computers and technology. She was one of the first people I knew who became connected to the internet."

Again I nodded.

"She would rather visit a library than go to a party."

"Yes."

"If she gets over-socialised she becomes quite wobbly."

"Yes."

"She doesn't like girly things, like shopping for clothes with friends. She doesn't believe she has to fit into any of the normal female conventions."

"Yes."

"She loves going to movies and reading fiction. They are a form of escape."

I nodded.

"She is so well-organised it freaks people out. She always needs to know what she's doing, where she's going."

"Okay, enough! What is this? It's like you're talking about me exactly."

"Don't get upset." She put her arms around me. "Aunt Lily is one of my very favourite people. I thought she was unique, but I can see there is another of her. That makes you very special to me."

Do you know how I felt at that moment? I felt like when I was a still at school and the most popular girl decided to be friendly to me. I almost didn't dare breathe in case the illusion was shattered.

She brushed the hair from my eyes.

"You know that you and I have been given something special. Something amazing."

I looked at her, all mussed up from sleeping and lovemaking. She looked like a goddess of the film world.

"You feel the same way, right?"

There was so much I wanted to say but the words just wouldn't form. All my thoughts and feelings were swirling around, flung like paper bags in the wind. I tried to catch some, articulate them, but all I could manage was to reach and cup her cheek with my hand. Then I leaned forward and kissed her lips.

"Just like my Aunt Lilly. I can see I'll have to do all the talking for both of us."

# CHAPTER THREE

I had until Monday to call the Boss but knew he was in the habit of visiting his office for a few hours on Saturday mornings. I wanted to get this conversation over with.

"Hey Janine. Did you enjoy your afternoon off?"

"Well, that's why I'm ringing. Something bad happened and I have to go away for a while."

"What? Why?"

"It's personal but I had to get away. I started driving west and I'm in Roma now."

"You're in fucking *Roma*?"

"Yes....I've got lots and lots of holiday leave as well as long-service leave. I'd like to take a large part of it. Sorry for the short notice. It just happened that way."

"So you've got the car as well?"

"Yes, and I'll need that. I'm sorry...."

"I wish you'd tell me what's wrong."

"Oh, well... I can't really. It's very personal. I just had to get out of town on my own. Can you do without me for a while?"

"Yeah, I guess so. How far are you planning to go?"

"I'll drive up the Matilda Highway from Charleville to Cloncurry, then go on to Darwin. From there I'll go down to Broome."

"Then what?"

"I have no plans after that."

"By the time you get to Broome you'll probably be sick of driving. You can arrange to get the car transported back by freighter if you want, and fly home. I'll pick up the charges."

"Thanks. If I decide to do that I'll let you know. Hey, I've got the laptop with me, so I'll need to send some files to whomever you decide to hand the work to."

We spoke for a while about how to split my workload. "You can always ring me if you need something special done. I've got the dongle as well, so can access the network."

"Okay, thanks but I'll try not to bother you. It will only be in an emergency."

"Thanks."

"Do you need any money?"

"No, I'm good thanks."

"You will let me know how you're going. I'll be worried."

 "Bye now Boss."

"Okay then, Stay safe. Call me if you need anything."

I could hardly see the "End" button for the tears in my eyes. Whenever anyone is kind to me I cry.


My choices of places to buy a good camera in Roma were very limited, but I knew it would only get worse the further northwest I went. There was an electrical store that boasted a range of digital cameras in their advertisement, but when I got there I found they were mostly the compacts. The best was a entry level DSLR kit with 75-300mm zoom lens which I purchased along with a tripod, carry bag, and other essentials.

I still had a long list of necessities to buy with limited places to source them. I ended up in a discount department store, part of a nationwide chain. I was happy there because it was a familiar layout and I knew I could get most of what I needed. The skincare and other toiletries were all the brands I used. I found some 100% cotton t-shirts, jeans, track pants, underwear and a jacket.

Every so often I'd feel myself crumbling. "Don't think

about it. Don't think about it," I'd say like a mantra. I'd shut my memory down and concentrate on the list in my pocket. Planning and organising were what I did best and if I kept myself busy I had a better chance of staying sane.

At the service station at the far end of the main street I filled the petrol tank and purchased the most comprehensive map they had. I also bought some containers for spare fuel and water. I checked my tyre pressure and cleaned the windscreen. I was in business.

The motel had a laundry for guests which I put to good use. I took all the labels from the clothing and ran them through a quick cycle. I tumble-dried what I could and used the clothes line for the rest. While they were drying I went back to the room and set up the camera.

By late afternoon I was well organised. I sat on the bed in my small room and looked around with satisfaction. My clothing and toiletries were all packed into a small, soft carry bag. I had the laptop case, camera case and tripod stacked together. I had ditched my handbag and purchased a small backpack that held my purse, mobile, sunscreen, tissues, mp3 player, lip-gloss, notebooks, map, and pens.

Then there was nothing else to do. I sat looking at the floor, feeling the cold fingers of sadness and distress gently lapping at my extremities, trying to find a way in to my body and mind. I reached for the motel phone and asked reception about the drive from Roma to Charleville. It was only a bit over three hours. I grabbed my bags and headed out the door.

The road was well sealed and fairly straight, excellent for high-speed driving. That was the good news. The bad news was that I was heading west in the late afternoon, so had the full strength of the sun in my eyes. The other bad news was that it was a stretch of the Warrego highway notorious for kangaroos that mostly hopped across the roads around sunset. I was annoyed at myself for not waiting until the next day to do this drive, but decided to relax and let whatever happened, happened.

I saw several kangaroos bouncing gracefully across the plains. Only one came close. It seemed to enjoy keeping parallel with my car and I slowed in case it decided to cross in front of me. Eventually it veered to the right and disappeared into the glare from the west.

My eyes were sore from the sun, even behind sunglasses, and no adjusting of seat position or sun visors would ease the discomfort.

I passed through tiny places called Muckadilla and

Amby. At Mitchell I remembered I wanted to swim in the Great Artesian Spa and slowed. The realisation that I hadn't yet purchased swimmers or goggles had me accelerating once more.

There was a town called Mungallala and then one called Morven. I saw signs to various tourist attractions but didn't want to stop, the feelings of velocity and continuity too seductive to give up for rare pre-historic rain-forests or historical museums.

I noticed the soil getting redder the further west I drove. I also saw the Mulga scrub take the place of grazing lands. Soon I was entering the township of Charleville and rummaged in my backpack for my notes on places to stay. I had originally vowed to only stay in historic outback pubs, but once I read the reviews of the ones in Charleville, I decided on a more modern Motor Inn. The best appeared to be two kilometres from the centre of town, a minor inconvenience. I wearily entered the address into the GPS and drove on.

It's rare for me to arrive at a hotel without a reservation, and now I'd done it twice in two days. I was shown to a nice room with a queen bed and air-conditioning. The pool looked inviting, and I made a mental note to buy some swimmers the next day.

Hanging my clothes only took a few minutes, after which the need to keep occupied overcame me again. I decided to drive in to town.

Walking into a strange pub alone is something way out of my comfort zone. I could feel the tension in my shoulders and the heaviness in my legs as I approached the bar.

"Hey, darlin'. What can I get ya?"

The barmaid was a heavily made-up woman, with deep creases and spider web wrinkles covering her face. Her hair was a mixture of blonde and grey and was pulled back harshly from her face. Her lipstick was bright red and looked incongruous.

"I might just have a light beer, thank you."

She took a wet glass from a tray on the bench and held it under an ornate tap which she pulled down, causing the beer to erupt in a creamy flow. I would have preferred it from a bottle, but it was too late.

"Here, dearie. What brings you into our corner of the world?"

This was one of my worst nightmares—a stranger wanting me to talk to them about personal matters. I mumbled something about 'just travelling through' and took my beer to an empty table by the wall.

Joe Cocker was playing. It sounded like a greatest hits album. A fly buzzed around my hair, and I swatted at it angrily.

There was a laminated menu wedged between some glass salt and pepper shakers. I scanned it, realising that I hadn't eaten since leaving Brisbane the day before. The thought of a pub meal wasn't a welcome one, but I decided to order something to fill my stomach. I ignored any sort of seafood, knowing it couldn't possibly be fresh that far from the coast. I saw lasagne and decided it was the best of a bad lot. I returned to the bar and waited for the barmaid to finish pouring drinks for two men who were indulging in some banter with her. She was laughing with a gleam of something in her eyes. What was that? Flirtation? I couldn't tell.

She wiped her hands on a soggy towel and walked towards me with raised eyebrows. I ordered the lasagne and returned to the table.

Both men watched me sit down and take a sip of beer. They talked between themselves, then said something to the barmaid. She looked at me and shrugged her shoulders. The younger-looking of the two men stood and came over to my table.

"My friend and I have decided to make your day. We're going to honour you with our witty and intelligent conversation while we ply you with alcohol. What do you say?"

It always takes me a minute to process a speech like this. There's so much subtext. What was he really trying to say?

I felt my forehead wrinkling.

"Hey, we're pretty harmless guys. Hey, Tom.....come over here and meet...er...what's your name?"

"Janine."

"Hi Janine. I'm John and this is Tom. We work together and are staying the night. What are you drinking?"

"Light beer."

John sat down while Tom went back to the bar to order drinks.

"We're staying in this hotel tonight. Are you?"

I shook my head. "Bad reviews."

"Ah, but such character! I've stayed here before. It's okay, except for the odd cockroach or two."

I shuddered and he laughed.

"So what's a beautiful thing like you doing in a place like this?"

"Just travelling through."

"Where are you headed?"

"Darwin, then Broome." I felt like I was being interrogated, and he had a way of trying to stare into my eyes that I found disconcerting. I decided to deflect the conversation away from myself.

"You say you work together. Doing what?"

"Ha! You'll love this. We're greeting card salesmen. I'm on my normal run and Tom is my area manager. He comes along once every year or so."

I nodded. I couldn't think of anything to say. I could always use him for information.

"What should I see while I'm here?"

"The big attraction is the Cosmos Centre. Astronomy at its best. The show starts at seven-thirty every night. It's great."

"What else?"

"Er...dunno. The tourist centre might be able to tell you."

The barmaid appeared suddenly and put my lasagne on the table with a crash that made me jump. She followed that with the cutlery, wrapped in a serviette. I thanked her, but she strode off without a word.

John smiled. "I think she'd been enjoying our company. You took us away, so you're a bad girl."

"Oh...."

Tom returned with the drinks, and I looked at the lasagne with distaste. It was served with greasy chips and a limp salad. I pushed it away.

"Not to your liking?"

"I guess I'm just not hungry. Help yourselves."

The men reached over and took some chips. Tom dipped his in the lasagne.

I downed my first beer and reached for the second. "Thanks for the drink."

Tom smiled. "No problems. I'll get you another on the next round."

"That's nice of you, but I'll be going soon."

"Where to?"

"Just back to where I'm staying."

"What are you going to do there?"

"Don't know. Sort out my gear. Do some washing."

"John and I must be losing our touch. Did you hear that, John? She'd rather go and wash clothes than talk to us."

John looked down and shook his head. "I'm shattered."

"Talk some sense into her. I'm going to talk to Jim over there."

Tom took his beer to the other side of the bar, and John leaned forward and tried to stare into my eyes again.

"You're not really leaving us, are you?"

I let out a deep breath. These men were confusing me. What did they want?

"I suppose you want me to have sex with you," I blurted out.

He sat back in his chair, his eyebrows raised to his hairline.

"Well....hello! You sure don't beat around the bush. Yeah...of course that's what I want."

I knew from history that it is hard to recover from one of those ridiculous faux pas of mine. I could either be terribly embarrassed or brave it out. I thought quickly.

"And you've got your own room here?"

"That's right."

The thought came from nowhere. "It'll cost you."

"Eh?"

"Sex. It will cost you."

"Cost me what?"

"Money."

"Eh? How much?"

What would an experienced hooker charge? I didn't have a clue.

"Two hundred for one hour."

"What do I get for that?"

"Standard sex."

"I don't need to pay for sex. I can get it anytime."

I shrugged my shoulders and sat back, sipping my beer. I'd braved it out and won.

"What do you mean by standard sex?"

"Vaginal penetration. With condom. In your room."

"What if I just want you to.....well.....do oral?"

"No oral. Hand job $100."

He was still frowning. "Wait here a sec. I'll be right back."

He and Tom went into a huddle for a few minutes. Tom opened his wallet and gave him some money.

I felt his hand on my shoulder. "Let's go."

The following is what I wrote from John's hotel room:

*The room is old. Not old-fashioned or historic looking, just old and tired. Nothing is fresh. Even the bed linen and towels look like they've been around way too long.*

*The air conditioner is turned down to very cold and makes strange noises from time to time. I'm sitting on an old, vinyl chair. It's green and heavy. The vinyl looked uncomfortable, so I laid a towel on it before sitting down, naked, to write this.*

*John is tangled in the bedclothes, noisily asleep. He's been that way for at least fifteen minutes now. He's one of those men who climaxes, and then becomes comatose immediately. I had to push him off me, an act that caused the condom to fall off him and land thickly on the sheets. I went to the basin and washed, bringing back a tissue to collect the condom, which I flushed down the toilet. His two hundred dollars is in my backpack. Somehow I knew the right way to collect money for sex. You always did it beforehand. How did I know that?*

*Did I also subconsciously know what the benefits of making sex a financial transaction would be? It meant we didn't have to go through the polite 'getting to know you' phase. It meant that John became only the third man in my life to have sex with me and I didn't have to give anything in return.*

*My watch tells me I still have twenty minutes of John's hour to go. If he paid for an hour I'm honour bound to wait until his time is up. The intercourse wasn't satisfying for me, of course. He had absolutely no finesse, but that was okay. He had taken my mind off everything for a while and I feel warm from having him inside me. I'm touching myself there now. Hmm that's nice…*

*I'm back. I've just finished giving myself a soaring, roaring orgasm. One of the best I'd had in years. It was exciting, facing him with my legs apart, thinking he could wake at any moment and watch me. I flew for ages, feeling the waves of pleasure wash over me again and again. It was hard to stay quiet.*

*At this moment I feel very calm and relaxed. The monsters have retreated to a far off land.*

*I'm going to sit here for a while longer and then get dressed and take more of a drive around town. This was good for me. I might do it again sometime soon.*

# CHAPTER FOUR

It was my first husband, Peter, who told me about the Matilda Highway. He wanted to travel its whole length, from the North of New South Wales all the way up to Kurumba, where Queensland meets the Arafura Sea. He planned to buy a used four-wheel-drive and refurbish it. We would take several months to explore the outback and be home before the baby arrived.

Our marriage didn't last long enough.

We were both from the same rural region of Victoria, a place where everyone knew everyone else and they all knew each other's business. No one else had really asked me out properly before Peter. They'd flirted and hinted; looking back I can see that now, but Peter spelled it all out properly and in simple terms. "I like you and I want to take you to see a movie on Friday night." He was wearing his leather biker jacket and looked different to the other boys, most of whom smelled of cows.

I went out with him, and it was okay. I didn't do or say anything awkward, and he held my hand in the cinema. We went out again the following night, and I lost my virginity in the back of his father's car. There were several more weekends of dates until I discovered the reason why my period was late.

As I say, everyone knew everyone else and they all knew each other's business. If you fell pregnant without a husband it was a catastrophe. There were huddled meetings of parents, dates set, and a walk down the aisle, dressed in white, all within a few weeks. All prayed that the baby would be as overdue as possible, and then the neighbours and fellow church members would be told it was a few weeks 'premmie'. Nobody was fooled, but they all played the game.

In my case, I was rushed up the church aisle to Peter's arms for no reason. Around month after the wedding I had a late miscarriage, on a witching no-moon night. Was I distraught? No. I hadn't wanted to be a mother and was relieved to find it wasn't going to happen. The dilation and curettage was the worst part of the whole thing. When it was over I returned home to look at Peter with a jaundiced eye.

I had gone from my childhood bed to Peter's overnight, with no time to discover the world on my own. I had never been independent. Worse than that was the fact that he always seemed to be there. I had no time alone. I was being driven mad.

His friends saw our home as a drop-in place. They would bring a six pack of beer and watch the football, cricket, or motor-racing. The lounge room would be constantly full of loud people expecting to be fed and entertained. I shrivelled inside.

My plans for finishing school and going on to tertiary studies had been thwarted by my pregnancy and marriage. I took a job as a book-keeper for a small company, but soon became bored with it. I saw a new position advertised, still clerical but working with computers, that excited me. I applied and was accepted. It was more than an hour's drive from home.

That drive every day saved my sanity. I was alone, listening to music I loved, as free as a bird. I can still remember the joy of climbing behind the wheel and hearing the engine fire. Kilometre after kilometre would pass before I merged into the peak-hour traffic, and until then I would be full of the wonder of nature's early morning gifts. One foggy morning I saw the bushy red tail of a fox disappearing into the green bush beside the road. Another time there was a duck, leading tiny ducklings from one dam to another, crossing the dangerous road to do so.

Often, as I neared home in the evenings, I'd feel my foot ease up on the accelerator, seemingly without any conscious thought to do so. I would pull into a quiet laneway and reach for my notebook. My mind would be fresh from the drive and I would spend at least half an hour either jotting down new ideas I'd thought up during the journey, or doing random writings. Sometimes it would be some poetry, sometimes just a dump of things on my mind.

The job was going very well and I was proving to have a natural talent with the computer system. I was given more and more responsibility and pay increases.

One day I overheard a co-worker talking about a granny-flat behind his place that had just become vacant since his daughter's wedding. It sounded amazing and was only fifteen minutes from work. I viewed it at lunchtime and did a deal on rent.

I told Peter I would just stay there during the week—that the long drives were too much for me. I took some of my things and settled happily into my little nest. I resumed my fiction writing, loving the quiet evenings. I started going into work on Saturdays when the computers weren't being used to establish a maintenance program I created myself. I'd arrive back to Peter late on the Saturday afternoon and leave earlier and earlier on the Sundays, saying I wanted to avoid the end-of-weekend traffic.

"It's not working, is it?" Peter's voice was deep and the words came slowly. He was standing at my car door, trying to delay my departure. "I think you're slowly leaving me."

I didn't know what to say. I shrugged.

"Do you want to take the rest of your stuff with you now?"

A dog came up and started sniffing at his boots. A cow bellowed in the afternoon air. A light rain began to fall.

"Okay."

There wasn't much left to take. Some books, music and old clothes. We were renting our house. I had my own bank account. I took my car and he kept his. It was over that easily.

I was alone at last.

Sometimes I get very annoyed with myself. This was one of those times.

I left Charleville early in the morning, bound for Longreach. It was a drive that should have taken around five hours. I had all day to cover this distance and planned to stop along the way to take photographs. I also planned to stop at pubs for breaks and lunch. It was a personality quirk of mine, however, that when I had a task to do, I just did it. If I had to drive from Charleville to Longreach, then I'd get behind that wheel and I'd drive. No stops.

I flew past Augathella and then Tambo. Was there anything to do there? I don't know. They were just a blur. On the approach to Blackall I had an argument with myself and decided to stop. There had to be something interesting to see and do. I fired up the laptop, but found I couldn't get signal on the broadband dongle.

My fingers drummed on the steering wheel as I overcame the itch to start the engine and keep driving. In the distance I could see a sign with the tell-tale yellow 'i' on a blue background which indicated there was tourist information available. Okay then, decision made. I climbed out of the car and walked to the Blackall Visitor Information Centre, which was housed in an old-style building with a large veranda along one side. It was manned by two middle-aged women who were delighted to tell me all about the region. I didn't have to say much at all. They handed me maps and brochures, marking items of interest in pink highlighter. I walked out feeling giddy.

Blackall is home to the Woolscour. This is operated by steam, and apparently is quite miraculous, but not my sort of thing. It is also the home of the Black Stump, and the Jackie Howe memorial. Mr Howe was apparently a fast shearer of sheep.

More wonderful than anything else was the aquatic centre with the artesian spa. I found a department store in the main street and bought a one-piece swimsuit. Not long after that I was lounging in the spa, relaxing my muscles. Then I did a few laps of the fifty metre pool, finishing with another dip in the spa. I felt brand new. What's more, I felt hungry for the first time in days.

The Barcoo Hotel in the main street was a large, rambling place with a camping ground at the rear. Although it was barely noon, the bar was crowded with all sorts of people, locals and tourists alike. I could see through to another, quieter area off the main bar and quickly made my way there.

I was pleased to find a selection of sandwiches on the menu and tried to find a way to order them. This meant going through to the main bar again. The barmaid looked like a clone of the one in Charleville, so I felt like I knew her, which is good for someone like me. Before talking to her, I thought about how the conversation would go and concentrated on being friendly.

"Hello there, ducks. Want some lunch, do yer?"

I smiled. I made sure the smile made it to my eyes. "Yes, please. I would like the assorted sandwiches on wholemeal bread, no butter. Thank you."

"No butter? Do ya want margarine then, love?"

"No, nothing thanks."

She sighed. I could hear her thinking, "City folk. All weird."

"Okay, I'll tell the kitchen. A drink to wash it down?"

"A light beer. From a stubby."

She nodded slowly. I paid, and she gave me a number on a stand. I told her I'd be in the quieter room.

"Ah, sorry lovie. We're not serving in there at the moment."

"Okay, that's fine. After you serve it, can I take it in there?"

"Yeah, okay. Bring your plate back, would ya?"

"No problem."

I looked around for an empty table. There was none. An old man waved at me, indicating that I could share his. I smiled and walked toward him, and as I did, he put a pen and notebook away in his breast pocket and stood to greet me. I was instantly impressed by his good manners. I was sure it was a rarity in the outback.

Our introductions were brief, and soon he had me fascinated by his rhythms of speech and methods of description. I found out he lived locally by choice. "I am an escapee of the cities and all they contain," he said with a glint in his eye. He asked where I was from and where I was going. This was done gently, and I didn't mind his questions. He also didn't stare into my eyes. He began talking about himself and I discovered he was a really interesting character. By the time my food arrived, I didn't want to go back to the quiet room. I offered him a sandwich, which he politely accepted. His name was Andrew Potter.

Although elderly, he was a man who held himself well. He didn't slouch or lean his elbows on the table. He sat straight and kept his shoulders square. He was dressed casually, as most were in the bar, but his clothing was clean and well-ironed. He still had a fairly good head of snow-white hair. The creases in his face seemed to be of the good kind, from smiling and laughing. His eyes were lively and dark, his skin brown from the sun. He wasn't a big man, but had a well-proportioned smaller build.

He was well spoken, too— none of the dropped h's and drawls common to central Australia. His was an educated accent. He spoke with a voice still full of strength. It lacked the breathlessness so common in the elderly. I was very impressed by him. In the two hours that followed I was given the gift of this remarkable man's story, and I was sorry when it came to an end.

People don't normally talk to me much and I assume it's because I give the impression of wanting to be left alone. For some reason Andrew broke through this. Was it because he was an elderly man who liked to talk? Was it because I'd changed? Maybe in my traumatised state I had become more open to humanity, to wanting to hear about the human condition. Perhaps he picked up on this. His personal history unravelled without any prompting by me, and I'm glad it did.

He told his story well, but in pieces that jumped backward and forward though his years. Sometimes I had to ask him for more information, wanting to understand how his mind worked and what had led such a cultured man to retire to the outback.

I'm going to retell Andrew's story, but will make one change, which is to put it in order and tell it in a linear fashion from his birth to the present time.

# ANDREW'S STORY

Andrew was born in France to Jewish intellectual parents who named him Andre. He was an only child. They lived in Paris in a sun-filled apartment and had a housekeeper called Marie. His earliest memories are happy ones of doting parents and a caring housekeeper.

He was too young to know about or understand the roundups of Jews that began in 1941. Life went on as normal for him, so he doesn't remember his life changing around that time. History shows that the earlier roundups, and most of the subsequent ones, were of Jews from other countries who had taken refuge in France, not the French Nationals, who were largely protected.

His luck, and that of his parents, ran out in early 1944. French authorities were under pressure from the occupying Germans to increase the quota of Jews being captured and deported. There was a roundup of known intellectuals and 'men of letters'. The housekeeper, Marie, did her best to protect them by suggesting she smuggle them to her parents' farm, outside of Paris. Andrew's father decided he wouldn't allow her or her family to endanger themselves on their behalf.

At this stage they were very ignorant of the ultimate fate of those who had been captured. They knew they were interned at places like Drancy, and that many were moved on from there. They didn't know about the death camps.

They were told to collect their papers and present them to a police station nearby. Father and Mother did so, leaving Andre in the care of Marie. They were told to go back and get him, however, and they complied.

The three were taken to Drancy Internment camp in March 1944. His parents were separated on arrival, but for a short time Andre was allowed to stay with his mother. That changed within a week, when he was taken from her and put in a building which housed only children. As he was pulled from his mother's arms he wasn't to know it was the last he would see of either of his parents.

"I now know they were deported to Auschwitz in a large shipment on May 20th and gassed on arrival," he said. "Very few survived that shipment." He stared at his hands and cleared his throat. "I wasn't sent there until July 31st

1944. Not that I knew the date then; I found out later. It was the last shipment from Drancy to Auschwitz."

On arrival there he was set to work, dragging corpses from the gas chambers, terrified of finding his parents among the dead.

"Auschwitz was liberated by the allies on January 27th 1945. I don't know how I survived until then, but I did. I was fifteen years old."

He was given papers indicating his status as a refugee and spent time in a displaced persons' camp. There he was fortunate to team up with a mother and daughter from Paris. The three of them eventually left the camp and returned to Paris together. "We didn't stay long". He looked in vain for Marie, knocking on the door of his parents' apartment, only to find it owned by another family. "They were less than pleased to find me at their door. I was moved on quickly."

On his sixteenth birthday he decided to take one of the refugee boats to Australia. There were agencies set up to take care of Jewish refugees, and he was glad for their help in relocating him. It took some time to organise and some time to get there, but he arrived in Sydney before his 18th birthday.

He had regained his health, and although conditions

on the boat hadn't been wonderful, he spent a lot of time up on deck, helping the crew. One in particular was kind to him and taught him English.

Andre was intelligent and resourceful. He quickly found that there was good money to be made at Mt Isa, and headed there almost immediately. There was a lack of young male workers due to the war, so he was given the job of a truck driver very quickly.

"The next fifteen or so years were almost a blur. In order to merge successfully into the Australian culture I changed my name to Andrew Potter. I worked long hours and saved my money, enough to buy a used truck. I then became a contractor to the mines and worked longer hours. Soon I was able to buy a second truck and hire a driver. By the time I was 35 I owned a fleet of forty trucks and was considered a successful man. By the age of forty I was very wealthy."

He assured me that he liked girls and found them attractive but hadn't the time or energy during those years to woo a girl. Also, there weren't many single women in Mt Isa, and in his first few years there it was clear that he was a refugee and therefore not considered a good prospect. He worked hard at losing his accent, educating himself, and learning to 'have a beer with the blokes' to become more

Australian.

"On my fortieth birthday I decided to find myself a woman and make a family. I had missed out on a normal childhood and wanted to experience it through children. My money helped. I started spending time in Brisbane and Sydney, donating large sums to the Arts. Soon the eligible women were swarming like flies in the outback." He stopped to swat a fly. We both laughed.

She had to be a lot younger than him of course. He finally met and fell in love with a self-assured woman of twenty-eight. They were married within six months.

"I now know that wealth attracts a certain type of woman. She is all soft and loving on the outside; she appears to be interested in everything you are. She hangs off your every word. Underneath this exterior is a hard centre, as I was about to find out."

They were blessed with twin boys before their first anniversary. His wife, Angela, hired a nanny to raise them, much to the horror of Andrew who pictured a close, nurturing family. Angela wasn't interested in the trappings of motherhood, however. She wanted to continue the lifestyle she had always enjoyed: the races, parties, opera, theatre, and fine dining.

"I spent more time with the boys than she did. My

business didn't require much of my time anymore. I had an excellent team of managers and moved my office to our house in Sydney. I would fly out to Mt Isa twice a week, but I was always impatient to be home with my boys."

He admits now that he spoiled the boys badly. He catered to their every whim: the latest toys, the biggest parties, and all too soon, the cars they wanted. He sent them to the best schools and on to university.

"I was so proud of my boys. They were handsome and charismatic. They weren't overly intelligent but applied themselves to their studies and succeeded where and when they wanted to. One studied business and the other marketing. They had the world at their feet."

His marriage was not a happy one, but Andrew was content with his family life. This all changed as the boys became adults.

"They gained their degrees but then couldn't seem to do anything worthwhile. They got good positions but weren't able to settle working for an employer. One was dismissed and the other left, both within one month of each other. They found other positions, but both failed again. It seemed they were useless at making a life for themselves. They were experts at living at home, partying, and dating a bewildering number of young women who all looked alike to me."

The situation worsened. It was becoming obvious that they were unemployable. They were lazy and aimless. Punctuality wasn't important to them. Lifestyle and holidays were. They soon attracted bad reputations and couldn't find decent positions anywhere.

"That's when they decided to go into business for themselves. Their dear old Dad was going to give them the money, of course. My wife thought this was a splendid idea, and the three of them ambushed me in my study one afternoon. They told me what they wanted to do, and how much money they needed." He paused and took a sip of his drink.

"It was a large sum. I surprised them by saying that if I did give them this amount, it would be as a loan. I surprised them further by asking for a business plan. They both looked at me with bewilderment. This wasn't going to be as easy as they first thought. They huffed out of my study, and then my wife started on me. I could afford it, she argued. Just give them the money. I was beginning to see what damage I'd done to these boys, and was keen to undo it. They had to learn about the realities of life, to stand on their own feet.

"Their next move was to go to my bankers behind my

back and ask them for a loan. The manager rang me, of course. We had a discussion, and I made my position clear—I would not stand behind this loan. The bank manager asked the boys for a business plan, a suggestion which was met with hostility."

They eventually secured a loan. It was at a high interest rate due to the lack of security. They started the business, and it floundered within a year.

'By then no-one was talking to me at home. None of the three of them had any respect for me whatsoever. If I wasn't handing out money to them I was invisible. It got to the point where they were getting ruder and ruder to me, all three of them. I knew my wife was giving the boys plenty of money to help them out of their circumstances, and this knowledge was making my blood pressure rise. I started spending more time back at Mt Isa."

His next move was the most fascinating part of the story.

"I finally made a decision on my 65th birthday. It was a quiet day; I was home for the weekend and there was only silence from my family. No birthday greetings, presents or celebrations. I was sitting in my study, going through paperwork, when I made a discovery that changed all the rules. One of my darling sons had stolen a cheque and forged my signature."

The devastation caused by this discovery was clear on his face, fifteen years later.

"A large national transport company had been wooing me for some time. They wanted to buy me out. We began discussions in earnest, and I sold my company to them. I then liquidated all my other assets, except for the house in Sydney. I worked out what sort of allowance my wife would need. I then purchased a small place just outside of town here and worked out how much I'd need to live on. Then I donated the rest to various charities."

He sat back and laughed. "You should have seen their faces when I told them! I had called my wife and sons into the lounge room for a 'family discussion'. I outlined what I had done and their faces were so comical that I started to laugh. They thought this was a sign that I was joking, so they started laughing too. Then I told them I was serious and showed them the paperwork.

"My wife lived on in the Sydney house, but on a reduced income, which meant the boys had to support themselves. They have done so, in a fashion. It's been hard, but they've had to adjust."

I asked him if he was happy where he was.

"Oh, yes. I have my small house and garden. I grow all

my own vegetables and herbs. I cook to please myself - I still retain a Frenchman's love of good food. I listen to classical music. I don't own a television, but am connected to the internet and have a good computer. A woman comes by once a week to do the heavy cleaning. I could do it, but have chosen not to."

When I asked him if he had a defining moment during his long years that changed his life he nodded.

"Two actually. There was the one I told you about when I found my son had stolen a cheque and forged my signature. The other is harder to explain." He shifted in his seat, cleared his throat, and looked over my shoulder into the distance.

"I was on the ship on the way here to Australia. I can't say I was happy back then. I was not yet eighteen years old, but had witnessed things that made me feel old. It was a heaviness of spirit, a weariness I couldn't shake. I was heading for a grand adventure, but couldn't feel a young man's joy of it.

"One morning I went to find my friend who was teaching me English. We would meet on the upper decks early in the day, not long after sunrise. I was early and found myself alone, watching a huge orange sun rising from the sea. The sky was clear except for some white streaks near the horizon. The air was filled with a glow. There was a stillness to the air that seemed not of this world.

"I stood and breathed in this special air. I felt close to the mysteries of the universe. Suddenly I could feel my parents close by - in this air. I felt their love - felt it enfold me. For those few precious seconds we were reunited.

"Until that point I didn't know their fate. It was assumed they had died in one of the extermination camps, and eventually I received official confirmation. As I stood on the deck of that ship, I knew without doubt they had left this earth and were reaching out to me, telling me of their love. The feeling passed within minutes, but I feel a comfort when I think of it." He was smiling at the recollection

"It was then that I decided to cast off the sadness and guilt."

"Guilt?" I asked.

"So many died: children, young adults, the elderly. I survived and yes, I felt guilty for that, but at that moment I cast that off. I decided that I owed it to those who lost their lives to live mine to the full. I decided to become healthy, wealthy, and happy. I would be one who escaped the horrors and not let it ruin my life."

"And you succeeded wonderfully."

"To a point. I made a mistake with my family. I've thought about this often, wondering if you can love too much, if you can give too much love. Then I realised my mistake was not that. You can't give too much love. What I did was give too much in the way of material comforts. I think my experiences in the holocaust caused me to do that. If I had my time over again, I'd do it differently."

He was silent for a moment. "But maybe it wasn't my experiences that caused me to do that. Maybe I just spoiled them as many people do to their children. Great wealth can be a bad thing. Yes, a person can have too much wealth and it can destroy the ones he loves - a bit like King Midas, perhaps."

He fell silent again. "Yes, I think that's it. There's a lesson in there, isn't there?"

# CHAPTER FIVE

Longreach was still two and a half hours away, and I wanted to stop at Barcaldine. That wasn't a problem; it was only two-thirty, but I didn't want to be driving at dusk again, with the threat of hitting kangaroos, so after shaking Andrew's hand and taking his photograph, I ran back to the car and roared out of town.

The uneventful drive from Blackall to Barcaldine only took a little over an hour. If there were any towns along the way, I missed them.

I spent the driving time thinking about my father. Andrew Potter caused that to happen, because I felt more warmth from that lovely old man in two hours than I ever had from my remote father.

Mum and Dad sold the farm in Victoria and retired to Queensland. Dad had a thing about North Stradbroke Island and wanted to buy a house there. They rented a place for the first twelve months so they could learn more about the area and real estate values. Point Lookout was Dad's choice. They waited for a suitable property to come on the market.

In the meantime, Mum developed a bit of a heart problem. Then she started having 'episodes', which we later found out were minor strokes. She spent time in hospital in Brisbane - there wasn't one on North Stradbroke Island - and then had to travel backwards and forwards to see specialists. To do so, they had to drive to Dunwich to catch the ferry to Cleveland, which was still half an hour's drive to the hospital. Then they'd have to do the same in reverse. One appointment took a whole day and cost a great deal of money.

Soon she began having kidney problems and the whole situation worsened. In a health crisis there were no facilities on the Island. Dad's dream of living there evaporated, and he didn't take it with good grace.

Mum didn't want to rent a house anymore. She wanted to own the house they lived in. They bought a small place in Chermside, a northern suburb of Brisbane. It had a nice rose garden and an old fashioned fence and gate. It was pretty, and Dad hated it. What's more, he let everybody know he did.

Mum died of a major stroke within six months of the house purchase. After we buried her, Dad sold the house at a loss and purchased one on "Straddie" which was extremely basic. He then proceeded to become one of those grumpy old men that you know to avoid at all costs.

My sister lives in Melbourne with her family. To visit Dad, she makes an annual migration, husband and kids in tow, and rents a holiday house where she does all the same work she does at home, but in a different location. Despite this, she is still able to think of it as a holiday. Her husband goes fishing most of the time, and if she's lucky he takes some of the kids along. On a really good day he buys some meat and cooks a barbeque. The entire trip costs a lot of money and she has to save hard to do it. Any offers of financial help from me are gently declined.

Dad is easier to manage when there are other people around. During my second marriage, my husband David, son Michael, and I started to do the same as my sister and her family, and rent a place to coincide with their visit. I would go again six months later, usually by myself, or with Michael if I could bribe him, just to check that Dad was alright. The last of these visits was just after I left David. Chris wanted to go with me but I thought that there were at least two people involved who wouldn't be happy with the end result. I still hadn't really spoken to Dad about the marriage break-up and certainly not about the cause of it.

The day was windy and cold, so the ferry was only half full. It was a smooth crossing, despite some choppy little waves. Soon I was standing at Dad's door, banging hard. I must have stood there for five minutes before he finally let me in, grumbling as he did so. "I told you I was coming Dad, and I'm right on time." He just shook his head and mumbled something as he went through to the kitchen.

I hadn't drunk black tea for many years, but he always makes a pot full and pours two cups. I took a green tea bag out of my handbag and tipped the black tea out of the cup.

"What the hell are you doing? What a waste!"

"Dad, I've told you over and over again. I don't drink black tea."

"You should be grateful that I made it for you."

I didn't answer. He put some biscuits on a plate and carried it into the lounge room. The plate had been one of Mum's favourites, and I would have loved to have taken it home. I knew better than to ask for it, though.

The two hours dragged by. I heard Dad's complaints about everything, from politicians to ferry operators. He didn't have a positive word to say. He didn't ask how I was, or how my work was going. I tried to tell him things but he would look away until it was time to start complaining again.

Apparently he has friends on the island. They meet a couple of times a week at the hotel. I wondered if he acted the same with them, or if it was just family he was obnoxious to. Perhaps they were all grumpy old men, enjoying getting together to complain. Heaven help us.

When I stood and said it was time to drive to the ferry, the mood in the room lightened considerably. I kissed him goodbye and walked out to the car. He remarked on the make and model and asked me how much they cost. I told him and he just nodded.

I arrived early at the ferry and sat in the dry warmth of the car, watching employees from the ferry company lining up the vehicles in pouring rain. As I drove past one of the workers, he smiled and waved at me. I smiled back. I remember wondering what he saw when he looked at me. Was he attracted to me, or was he just being friendly? The relief of leaving my father made me optimistic. I decided to believe it was the former.

It wasn't hard to find a pub in Barcaldine. There were six lined up, all on the same side of the street. It was very quirky. They were all old-style pubs, the sort that you would expect to see a horseman ride up to. He'd climb wearily from his mount and tie the reins to the post, then brush the dust off his moleskins as he entered the bar.

I picked the Artesian Hotel, just because I had enjoyed the swim in the artesian spa earlier in the day. It was rough and ready, as I'm sure they all were, but cool and inviting to sit in. I was becoming more confident at talking to bar staff and remembered to be friendly and open with them.

This one was a middle-aged man, balding, with glasses on a chain hanging over a huge beer gut. I wondered how his legs could support all that weight. He sighed as he walked towards me.

"Yes, Miss?"

"A light beer thanks, in a stubby."

"Coming right up." He waddled to the huge, glass-fronted refrigerator and reached in for my order.

"Is there any food available at the moment?"

"Dunno. What do you feel like?"

"A sandwich, perhaps?"

"I'll ring through and see. Any particular sort?"

"Ham, tomato and cheese on brown bread? No butter

or margarine."

He looked levelly at me for a moment and picked up the phone. "Yes, that's right. No butter or margarine. I dunno, it's just what she asked for."

I took my beer further into the dim room. There were a couple of old-timers, each of them standing on one leg and resting the other on the metal bar that sat 50 mm or so above the floor. Their hats were tipped back on their heads and miraculously stayed in place when the men leaned back to down their beers.

I took a table towards the far wall. After a few minutes a young woman approached hesitantly.

"Do ya mind if I sit with you?"

I then realised how hard it is to sit alone in a pub in the outback of Australia.

I waved my hand toward the spare seat and she sat, looking at me with huge eyes.

"Yer not from around here, are ya?"

"No, I'm from Brisbane."

She looked around the bar then leaned forward. "I was wondering if you could tell me somethin'."

"Sure."

"If I went to Brisbane, would I be able to get, like, a ...a..termination?"

I frowned, searching my brain for any information that might be swimming there.

"Sorry....did I upset you by asking that? I 'eard there are people called "Right to Lifers" or somethin'."

"No, I'm not one of those. I just don't know the answer to your question. I can't even tell you if it's legal in Queensland. I have a feeling it's not."

Her shoulders sagged.

"I think it's legal in other states, though. Do you have access to the internet?"

She shook her head. "There's a computer at 'ome, but I dunno how to clear the history after I've looked. Someone could find out."

I looked at this girl closely. She was unusually pale for this part of the world and her eyes had dark rings under them. They were also very bloodshot. I made a decision.

"I'll go and get my laptop out of the car."

The dongle wasn't in range, but my mobile was. Different carrier. I used my smartphone as a wireless point and connected my laptop to it. I found a Wikipedia page which listed the legislation state-by-state. A quick scan of the information indicated that the best places to obtain an abortion were in Western Australia or the ACT.

I passed this information on and she nodded glumly.

"How far are you gone?"

"Nine weeks."

"Can you get to either of those places?"

"I dunno. I'll have to try to work it out."

"Can your local GP help?"

She laughed hollowly. "He's my 'usband's best mate."

I must have looked shocked. "You're married?" I looked at her left hand. A narrow yellow gold band sat on her ring finger.

She began crying. "It's not my 'usband's baby. I've gotta get rid of it before 'e realises I'm pregnant." She swallowed and hiccupped.

"What about your mother or father?"

I saw a tension in her jaw and a narrowing of her eyes. It was a hard and bitter look, which she struggled to hide. "Nah." she said as she dropped her gaze to the floor. I wanted to ask her about the father of the baby, but she'd closed down. No more information was forthcoming.

I slid the laptop over, and she sat down and started poking inexpertly at the keys. I went to the bar and ordered each of us a drink and on returning, moved another small table over near ours to put them on.

I could see she was getting frustrated, so I gently slid the laptop back and started a search. Within seconds the information was all there. As she looked at the screen I got us each another drink. She read slowly, but drank quickly. I noticed the tension leaving her face and body. She got to the bottom of the web page and sighed.

"I got no choice, you see? I just gotta get rid of it." Her eyes had a haunted look. For a few minutes she looked down at her hands, silently. She took a deep breath and raised her eyes to mine. "I can't have it, okay?"

"Okay."

Tears sprang to her eyes. "It's father....the father..," she was swallowing hard and hiccoughing. "I can't tell ya...I haven't told anyone."

I nodded and began packing up my laptop.

"You're not angry at me are ya?"

The question surprised me. "No, why?"

"I dunno. It just seems like you are."

"No. It's just none of my business."

I stood up, and she grabbed my hand. "Can't ya stay a bit longer?"

I smiled and shook my head. I explained that I was driving to Broome and needed to keep moving. I wished her luck and walked out the door.

# CHAPTER SIX

Longreach was still one and a quarter hours away. As I drove away, I thought about pregnancy. I recalled the changes to the body, especially hormonally. It would be hard for her to be going through such a crisis. It was hard enough even fully supported by a husband.

David, my second husband, decided one day that he wanted children. I suppose it's strange that I had never considered the possibility that he would want this. I guess it's normal for a man, or woman for that matter. I was different. The thought of being labelled as a mother left me cold. It was bad enough being David's 'missus'. I've always considered both wife and mother to be derogatory terms.

In any case, he wanted children, and the relationship was still new enough for me to want to please him. We discussed it at great length, and he finally convinced me that it would be good for us. He saw it as adding to our relationship. I saw it as inviting an interloper.

I stopped taking the contraceptive pill and thought I'd become pregnant quite easily. That didn't end up being the case. This came as a bit of a shock to me. Once I decide to do something, I do it, and I do it quickly and to the best of my ability. Month after month my periods arrived, heavier and more painful than when I was on the pill. We started visiting doctors and specialists. I began taking fertility drugs. The next move was a keyhole procedure to check out my internal organs.

I wasn't happy with this prospect. Although it was only day surgery, I felt like I would be out of control. To help me, David took me to the day hospital to have a look around a few days before the procedure. On the day it was to be performed, he took the day off work and stayed with me as long as he was allowed. When I woke from the anaesthetic, he was there, holding my hand. "They didn't find anything wrong," he said, proudly.

One month I thought we might have been successful. My period was a few days late, and I was feeling different. I dared to tell David and he was ecstatic. Later, however, I felt the beginning of cramps. There were spots of blood. I was distraught, and David and I drank half a bottle of Scotch.

The next morning I found that the cramps and bleeding had disappeared. I purchased a home pregnancy test and my hands shook as I read the result. Positive. I whooped with joy. I didn't tell David until I had it confirmed by the doctor. We were on our way.

I wasn't a good incubator for our child. I developed pre-eclampsia and blew up like a balloon. My kidneys weren't handling the pregnancy well. Finally I had to have an emergency caesarean at thirty-eight weeks, and Michael was born on the night before a full moon. Had I gone full-term, he would have been born at the time of a new moon. I decided it was better this way.

Was I a good mother despite my ambivalence? I believe so. I was as protective as a lioness is of her cub. I loved the smell of him and would bury my nose in his hair and the place where the shoulder meets the neck. I did all the right things. I breast fed him until my milk dried up at six months. The happiest times were when he became more interesting and could talk to me. We spent hours playing on the floor of our lounge room, building castles out of blocks and playing with dinosaurs. I read to him every night before he went to sleep, as well as any other time we had spare.

He started kindergarten and always ran through the door excitedly. I remember one rainy day we had run quickly from the car and arrived at the door breathless and giggling. A woman inside the door looked up and said, "Oh, here's Michael's mum!" I felt a coldness settle over me, the joy of the moment gone. I looked at the woman, saw her smile begin to falter, and wanted to tell her that I was Janine, not Michael's mum, not David's wife. Just *Janine*.

Seconds had ticked by, and I knew I was doing it again - alienating myself from other people. I forced a smile and stepped forward. I held out my hand and said, "Sorry, I was thinking about something else. I'm Janine. Whose mum are you?"

I saw the frown leave the woman's face. I saw the smile re-appear. The world stopped tilting crazily and everything was back to normal. Shortly after that I fled to the car and drove to the safety of my home. I ran upstairs to my writing room and grabbed a notebook and pen. Only after an hour of frantic scribbling did I begin to calm myself again.

Not far out of Longreach I passed through a town called Ilfracombe. I had meant to ask the barman about it in Barcaldine, but was diverted by the pregnant girl. The shadows were lengthening by the time I reached the town, so I didn't stop. I could tell, however, that there was a thriving sheep industry there.

I was happy to see the outskirts of Longreach. I figured it might be one of the highlights of the Matilda Highway. I'd done my homework and already knew what to see and do. All I had to do now was find a place to stay.

I knew there was a Motor Inn that had earned consistently good reviews. It was also reputed to have a good restaurant. I set the GPS to the address and arrived keen to stretch my legs. I thought I might also have a swim before dinner.

Luckily they had a vacancy, and I was directed to my room without fuss. I had washing to do and some notes to make. Other than that I could just relax. I sorted my clothes, changed into swimmers, and did several laps of the pool. Back at the room I rinsed the chlorine out of my hair and off my skin, then changed into fresh clothes. I did a load of washing and lay down on my bed for a while.

That was the trouble with filling my time with new experiences and new people. At some stage or another I had to stop. That's when all the bad returned, creeping with menace. Minutes later I was in the foetal position, sobbing my heart out. When I calmed down a bit I realised I should have a good book with me to divert my mind during resting times. Why hadn't I thought of that earlier?

Knowing that travellers often left books behind when they'd finished them, I asked the friendly person working at the reception desk if they had any. I had a choice of ten or so. None could be categorised as literary fiction, but there were some readable ones. I took two and gave the receptionist my heartfelt thanks.

I know my way around fine dining establishments, and the dining room at the Motor Inn was definitely not one. It had good, hearty food, however. Mostly it consisted of a cut of meat with vegetables or salad and a few soups. Country folk like their desserts, and there was a good range. I drank a glass of wine with my chicken and returned to the room. I sat in the chair and wondered what to do next. There was free wireless in the lobby, so I took my laptop there and connected to the internet. I spent some time looking at websites about Longreach, and also learned more about the trip onwards to Cloncurry. All the time I was doing this I could feel someone watching me.

He wore an ordinary, but good quality, jumper over what was obviously a uniform of some sort. He was sitting alone, nursing a drink. When I looked up at him, he smiled and lifted his glass. I smiled back.

A minute later he was sitting in a chair near mine.

"What can I get you to drink?"

"Oh, a white wine, thanks."

He disappeared into the restaurant and brought back two glasses. He handed me mine and raised his. "To new friends!" he said, and then clinked his glass against mine.

John Two worked for Qantas as a flight attendant. He was meant to fly back to Brisbane, but his flight had to be delayed until morning. I call him John Two because John One was in Charleville. I decided not to use their real names, for obvious reasons.

I decided to only charge him $150 dollars for an hour. Like John One, he originally baulked at the suggestion, but produced the money nonetheless. He also purchased a bottle of wine to take back to his room, which he carried in an ice-bucket with both hands, closing the door with a backward kick. He said he had cocaine and asked if I wanted some. I declined, so he disappeared into the bathroom and came out rubbing his nose.

This is what I wrote in his room:

*I suppose it was the drug that made him so energetic. He got his money's worth, I can tell you. He moved me into various positions and at one point it seemed he was going to try for some anal penetration. I moved slightly to divert him away, and he got the hint. He seemed to be able to contain his orgasm until a few minutes short of the hour. When he finished he lay back and patted the pillow next to him. I had been lying sideways, so moved, placing my head next to his. He began talking about his home life and then dozed off.*

*Now I'm sitting up in the bed. The two bedside lamps are on, as is the bathroom light which casts a soft, indirect glow onto the bed. John Two is breathing quietly. He doesn't seem to snore. I'd class him as a good and athletic lover, obviously fit and healthy. He lives with another flight attendant, a woman, and they have a relationship of sorts. Nothing serious, though, he was quick to add. I reckon she thinks it's more serious than he does.*

*It's time to dress and go back to my room. It would have been nice to curl up against him , but I want to wake in my own room. His skin smells nice to me which is unusual, and I've sniffed him a few times. Now I'll whisper good night and tip-toe out.*

# CHAPTER SEVEN

The Stockman's Hall of Fame was founded by artist Hugh Sawrey to create a memorial to the explorers, overlanders, pioneers, and settlers of outback Australia. It was opened by Queen Elizabeth II in 1988. I was told it was a 'must see', so I put aside my dislike of tourist attractions and went along.

I tried to slow down and have a good look at the relics on display, but I'm just not wired that way. The art works held my attention for longer, but I was still in and out of the place very quickly. At the shop I purchased a women's Akubra hat and two books: *We of the Never Never* and *The Heart Garden*.

The Qantas Founders Museum was more interesting to me. I had, in my teens, become a bit obsessive about aviation, and toyed with the idea of training for a pilot's licence. To be able to walk around the various aircraft, both historical and modern, at this museum was something I found fascinating.

Late in the day I had a light beer in a hotel on the main street, but it seemed mostly inhabited by tourists. I downed it quickly and moved off. I saw a small supermarket a few doors down and decided to pick up some supplies, including green tea, which didn't seem to be offered anywhere in the outback.

There was a queue at the checkouts, and I looked around at my fellow shoppers. The woman in front of me was aboriginal and had a young girl with her, probably her daughter. The girl looked up at me shyly, her huge brown eyes unfathomable. She smiled and buried her face in her mother's faded print dress. I smiled back at her.

Finally it was the aboriginal woman's turn to be served. She placed a two-litre bottle of milk and a loaf of bread on the counter. The check-out girl looked her up and down with a curled lip. I felt my hackles rise. The woman paid and walked out of the store. I made my purchase and followed. Outside, I found a kerfuffle.

The woman had been stopped by a middle-aged man wearing the supermarket uniform. He was rummaging through her handbag, removing items and shaking his head. I stood out of sight and watched. Only the little girl noticed me, and she played a game of hiding her face from me then looking again.

The man was talking loudly to the woman and waving his arms in the air. People in the street were slowing down to take in the spectacle. The man told the aboriginal woman to follow him into the store.

I walked up to them. "Excuse me. I know this woman. What seems to be the problem?"

He turned and looked me up and down. "The problem is that people won't mind their own business."

"Well that may be the case, but I'd genuinely like to help here."

"The police will help, thank you madam. Now if you'll be on your way—"

"Oh, getting the police involved is so time-consuming. I think it might be better if I pay what my friend here owes you, and we can all be on our way."

"No. She's not going to get away with this. We lose too much stock this way. We have to report these crimes."

"Crime? I'd hardly call it that. I'm sure there was a reason. Please, let me pay for the items and I'll take her off the premises."

His face began to soften.

"Please?"

We went to the service counter. The items, which just consisted of basic food essentials, were added up. It wasn't as though she was trying to rip off expensive items. The total came to $20.55. I handed over the cash, took her arm and walked out of the store.

"Let me buy you and your daughter some afternoon tea," I said.

I led them into a cafe and the three of us sat down. This must have been unusual, because we seemed to attract some 'looks'. The waitress hurried over and I ordered scones with jam and cream and an assortment of sandwiches. I also ordered a milkshake for the girl and a coffee for myself. The woman just asked for water.

I introduced myself and asked her name. "Jenny," she said, looking down at the table.

I asked the little girl her name, but she just hid her face again. "Suzie," said the mother.

Hearing her name, the girl began wiggling in her chair and chatting to herself. I took out my notebook and tore a page out. I handed it to her with a fine point felt pen and asked her to draw me something.

She wedged her tongue between large front teeth and began drawing lines.

For the second time since leaving Brisbane, someone

told me their story without any encouragement from me. Jenny began hesitantly, not by thanking me for helping her in the supermarket or anything like that, but in a circular way.

Now, as I sit with my fingers poised over the keys of my laptop, I find I am struggling to find the voice with which to tell her story. I realise I am totally unqualified to relate what she told me.

I remember how lost I was when she first began talking, telling me about numerous aunties and grand-mothers and it took me some time to realise that all these women weren't blood relations, that they were people in her life that would, from time to time, help her or be part of her life. This was only the beginning of the bewilderment I experienced.

She spoke of places I'd never heard of, and of events that only just stirred the slightest spark at the periphery of my memory.

My usual skill of being able to recall conversations word-for-word has deserted me. Her speech was full of strange rhythms and cadences that would not register in my mind for any length of time.

All I remember is the main storyline, so I feel I have already failed in the retelling of this story, and this is before

I have even begun recording it. Nevertheless, it is important that I try.

I have spent several hours researching much of what she has told me, filling in the blanks of my knowledge, so my retelling of her story will not suffer from ignorance.

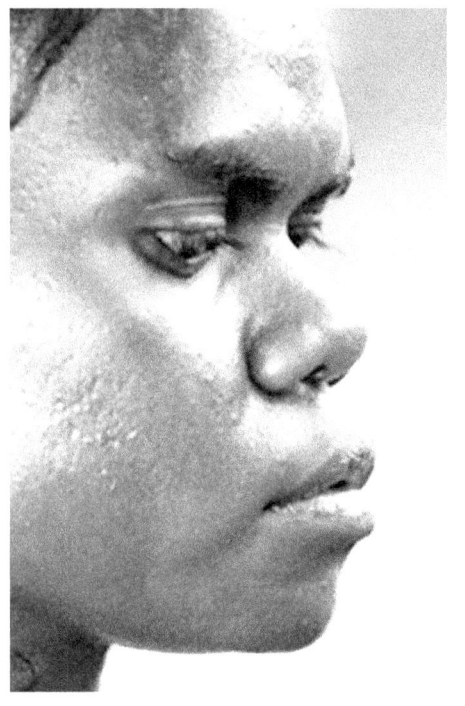

# JENNY'S STORY

Jenny was born and raised in an Aboriginal settlement called Yuendumu which is a three-hour drive northwest of Alice Springs. This settlement has, historically speaking, boasted a reputation for growing and developing a community of talented artists. It has also bred some excellent AFL players. Its schools and other community institutions are better than those at most settlements.

It also, however, has a drug and alcohol problem.

Jenny doesn't know who her father is. She and her two siblings were raised by their mother, an alcoholic, with some help from aunties. Sometimes these women would swoop in and gather the children up for the duration of one of her mother's benders.

Some of these aunties had their own problems, violent or abusive husbands being a common theme. The women would stick together and create safe houses, often at a grandmother's house, where men were not allowed, and where the women could stay until the 'sorry business' was over.

Jenny did very well at school and her teachers often sang her praises. They celebrated her intelligence at every opportunity, using her as an example of what could be achieved through hard work. Her older sister wasn't as good at school and began drinking, often in the mornings before school as well as in the afternoons. Alcohol wasn't hard to come by in their house.

Their mother sometimes went to Alice Springs by herself for several days. On one of these trips she met a man and decided to live with him. He was adamant he wouldn't live at the settlement, and in the end they decided to move to Darwin. Some violence had broken out at Yuendumu, so it wasn't a hard decision to make.

Living in Darwin was hard for Jenny. She missed her friends, and particularly her teachers. The new school was a mixed-race one and she didn't stand out as such a high-achiever. Her home life wasn't happy either. She'd heard her stepfather and older sister making noises in the dark while her mother snored in alcohol-induced oblivion. The stepfather had started to look at Jenny in ways that made her feel uncomfortable and would occasionally brush against her or attempt to grab a breast or buttock. One night he tried to climb into her bed, smelling nauseatingly of sweat, tobacco, and alcohol. She screamed and hit him until her older sister woke and began hitting him as well. She couldn't go back to sleep that night, and instead lay awake to plan her escape.

She was sixteen years old and felt she could return to Yuendumu settlement on her own. One of the aunties would house and feed her and she could return to her much loved school. She had little money, but raided her mother's then her sisters' purses, which only helped the situation slightly.

Early the next morning she walked to the main highway and pointed herself towards Alice Springs.

The first two truck drivers were nice men who shared their meals with her and made sure they dropped her in safe places. The third was driving a road train. He was younger than the other two, and Jenny found him attractive. He lived in Alice Springs and suggested that when they got there she stay with him for a few days before she attempted to find her way to the settlement. He hinted that he might even drive her there on a day off.

He lived by himself in a small flat. It didn't have much furniture, but was clean and tidy. There was only a double bed and a sofa for sleeping, and she offered to bed down on the sofa, but he insisted on sleeping there.

At one point during the night she was having a nightmare about her stepfather, when she felt someone sliding into the bed. This caused a violent reaction in her which the truck driver didn't take kindly to. She wasn't sure if she should label what happened next as rape because had she not been having the nightmare she probably would have welcomed his embraces.

She ended up spending several weeks in his flat and probably would have been there longer except for an unfortunate episode. One Friday night a mate of the truck-driver dropped in for a few beers. He saw her and later she heard the two of them talking in the kitchen. The mate asked if the truck-driver was into 'boong sheilas now'. That night he slept with his back to her and the next day asked her to leave. He didn't offer to drive her to the settlement.

She walked around Alice Springs for a few hours, trying to figure out the best way to catch a ride. She found some Kooris in a dusty park, their dogs and cars around them. There were several young men and two girls. Her intention was to ask how she could get to the settlement, but she ended up sitting with them all afternoon, sharing their beer. One of the boys was attractive and seemed unattached. She spent a lot of time talking to him.

Once again she didn't make it back to the settlement. She took up with the boy and his rough life-style. Although she had always resisted alcohol in her mother's house, it was part of the culture in this new group of friends and she felt a pressure to fit in. Soon she was drinking heavily and smoking cannabis.

When they ran out of money to support their various habits, some would perform break-and-enters of local homes. Sometimes her boyfriend would take part. Soon this also became part of her new reality.

As a result of this new lifestyle she found herself, at the age of eighteen, jailed and pregnant. It had all happened with bewildering speed, and in her alcohol and drug-induced haze she barely knew what had happened to her.

She was released from jail in time for the birth of her baby. Her boyfriend, who had run fast to escape arrest on the night she was captured, had taken up with another girl. Jenny was understandably upset and didn't know where to turn. The boyfriend came back to her, however, and after the baby was born, the two of them found a place to live away from the circle of friends they knew was a bad influence.

She was determined to stay 'clean' and be a responsible

mother. She wouldn't follow the same path as other Koori women, including her own mother, who Jenny now realised was a bad role model to her children.

Her boyfriend heard of a new job in Winton that would pay well, so they moved. Soon decent pay checks started appearing, and Jenny was proud of him, proud of her little family. Sadly it didn't last long before the boyfriend was drinking and taking drugs again. After one particularly bad week at work, where he was the victim of racial slurs and bullying, he got badly drunk and came home in a nasty mood. Jenny had seen this mood in others and knew what it led to. She said if he hit her or the child even once, she'd call the police and have him taken away. She'd also get a Domestic Violence Order against him. The words penetrated his addled mind and he didn't inflict any physical injuries on her or their baby daughter.

What he did do was verbally abuse her on many occasions. Sometimes she thought this was harder to take than a beating. He would get nasty and sarcastic. He would call her a whore and a slut. Sometimes he would do this when they were outside in the street, accusing her of having sex with their neighbours. Any self-esteem she had was draining away. Finally she summoned all her strength and told him if the abuse continued she would leave him and take their child.

For several weeks he was affectionate and non-abusive, but one night he came home drunk and it all started again. She contacted a local group who helped in such cases, and they found her and her child a place of their own to live in.

On the day I met her, her welfare payments hadn't kicked in. The money promised by her boyfriend hadn't materialised. She had gone to the supermarket desperate for food but with little cash. It was the first time she'd even thought of stealing since being released from prison. She knew it was stupid and knew if she got caught she'd end up back behind bars.

My intervention with the security person had saved her this fate and had made her realise how close she'd been to losing her child.

"Town is no good. I see what happens to Koori peoples here. I gotta get me and me baby back to Yuendumu. This time I *gotta* make it back."

She hoped the same teachers were still there, the ones who encouraged her and made her feel good about herself. She planned to see them in the hopes they could give her advice on how to further her education before it was too late.

When I finished this story I sat back in my chair and tried to imagine being Jenny. I tried to explore her psyche in an attempt to understand her thought processes and emotions. I tried to feel the lack of choices she suffered from and the limitations she felt were imposed on her. Finally I blew out my cheeks and decided it was too hard. I don't think that in the whole of my life I have even spoken to an aboriginal - not through choice, you see. Just because I had never had the opportunity. I am totally clueless.

As we walked out of the cafe into the hot street, I asked Jenny if she'd mind if I took her photograph. She shrugged. I sat her down on a bench and took several shots close up. Her face was amazing.

I opened my backpack and took out the three hundred and fifty dollars I'd earned with the two men. "Here," I said and stuffed the notes into her hands. She just stood looking at them with wide eyes and raised brows. I tickled the little girl on the belly and walked away, smiling at the thought that I had just acted like a modern day Robin Hood, even though my methods of stealing from the rich were rather different.

In the few days since I left Brisbane I had heard two amazing life stories. I mused about the fact that everyone has a story; the old, the young, the poor, and the wealthy. All of us have experienced life both good and bad. There comes a time when these stories need to come out, need to be told to another human being. I thought about what a great book this would make. It would be a slim volume containing several stories and each would have a photograph of the person telling it.

I looked back and saw Jenny sitting on the bench, still looking at the money. I pulled out my notebook and wrote a few words as I walked back to her. She looked up with fear in her eyes, probably scared that I'd changed my mind about the money. I just smiled and explained what I'd come back for. I showed her the words in the notebook. She nodded. I asked her to sign. She did it slowly, with her tongue thrust out over her bottom lip. I smiled and walked away again.

I had just gained permission to tell her story. I wondered about Andrew Potter. I took out my mobile and dialled Sensis, asking for the number of the Barcoo Hotel in Blackall. I was banking on the fact that Andrew seemed like the sort of man who would go to the same pub at the same time every day. I was in luck. The barman put me through, and I had a short conversation with Andrew. I got an address to send a confirmation for him to sign, and as I ended the call I felt a sensation in my stomach that came from knowing I was creating something of importance.

# CHAPTER EIGHT

Back in my room I opened the laptop and created a Word document. I wrote Jenny's story first while it was fresh in my mind. It took several pages and I knew I would edit it later. Andrew's was a bit harder due to the complexity of his life, but by the end I was satisfied.  I finished with his answer to my question about the defining moment in his life. It was very poignant.

It was good to be writing again. I found the words came easily. Writing with a fountain pen and good quality paper was my preferred method, but in this case practicality demanded that I type it directly into the word processor. I wasn't inventing stories, anyway, just reporting them.

I thought about all the times in my life that writing had been a refuge. When life became too confusing, I could retreat into my fictional worlds where I had control over everything that took place, like a master chess player, bent over his board, sending royalty and their pawns into battle. Sometimes, though, my characters did unexpected things that delighted me. I would have the story mapped out in my mind, only to find a major character had taken a totally different course of action. At these times it was hard to break away from the writing, as I was fascinated to learn what was going to happen next.

I glanced over the two stories again, and then saved the file to a new folder on my desktop. I named it simply "Stories".

My urge to keep a photographic record of these people's faces was in my favour. I would look later at how they had turned out and save them on to my hard drive.

I thought about the young woman in Barcaldine. Hers would have to be an interesting tale. Shame she hadn't wanted to tell me. I didn't have a photograph of her anyway. Thinking about it made an image came to mind. A page, blank except for a roughly drawn smiley face - but the smile was upside down.

Opening a new Word document, I typed words similar to those I'd given Jenny to sign the hour or so before.

I didn't know if the wording was legal or not and didn't particularly care. I didn't think any of these people would cause me any grief in the future. I saved the document to a USB stick and took it to reception. They printed twenty copies for me. I wondered where I should get Andrew to post his copy back to. The woman on reception was fine with receiving it at the Motel, and with forwarding it if necessary. I mailed it to him there and then.

I was on my way.

I went for a quick early-evening swim and then a quiet dinner in the restaurant. Writing the stories down had caused a surge in my need to create. I was between novels, so there was nothing I felt the need to write. Instead, I took up my fountain pen and a fresh pad and started writing about my idea for the book and expanding on it. My fountain pen skimmed across the lines, as joyous and free as a cartwheeling child. I could have written all night. I stopped after five pages and at the end of them felt like a fitness junkie after a good hard run, tired but happy.

*We of the Never Never* was waiting for me on the bedside table. I had read it during my school years, but wanted to see it through the overlay of adult experience. I fell asleep after two chapters and slept soundly for seven hours.

# CHAPTER NINE

I sat in my SUV, biting a flap of skin on the inside of my mouth. Longreach to Cloncurry was a drive of nearly six hours. I was torn between doing it in one day and stopping at Winton overnight.

If I wanted to continue with my plan of writing this book, I'd need to slow down and spend a lot of time in public places, willing people to come to me and tell their stories. Talking to strangers wasn't something that came easily to me and the very thought of it made my stomach squeeze like a fist. The first two stories had just landed in my lap. Could more come to me as naturally?

I had heard of things like this happening to writers. The universe created a synchronicity, and then things just fell into place. I prayed this would continue to be the case. As I set my course to Winton, I decided to just see what happened.

The steady voice on the GPS started issuing instructions. I relaxed and began moving off, setting my radio to a local station as I did so.

Before long I was driving the Matilda Highway again, through the red dust of the mulga plains. The sun was bright, and I made a mental note to buy some better quality sunglasses. I pulled the sunshade down in an attempt to reduce the glare.

A song came on the radio that made me think of my second husband, David. It was "A Kiss from a Rose" by Seal. David hadn't really been into music, but this song had struck a chord in him, and he played it incessantly. It used to get stuck in my head and drive me mad.

I don't think badly of my second husband. I don't really think of him at all. What amazed me was how I allowed myself to be with him, to lose the precious freedom that I had fought to reclaim.

I was living in the lovely little granny flat in the Melbourne suburbs, and life was humming along. I had written two novels and was feeling good about myself. Life always presented challenges, but I was strong in my state of independence and was coping well. Then several major changes started to blow in with the cold winter winds.

The couple I was renting the flat from was getting plans drawn for a swimming pool and tennis court, which would mean the demolition of the granny flat. It wasn't going to happen immediately, but I was feeling the stress of knowing the impermanence of my situation. Also the husband was becoming a bit of a nuisance. He would appear from time to time, usually when his wife was out, and ask if I needed anything. The first few times I just said that I was fine and wanted for nothing. Then he began commenting on the fact I never had men around. Didn't I miss male company? It took a while for the penny to drop - hinting doesn't work with me; I just take words literally - but when I realised what he was hinting at I was appalled. I no longer felt safe and protected in my little haven.

At the same time I was becoming bored with my job. I

had learned a great deal and even did some external study in some computing subjects. The computer system was running without major glitches, mostly due to the weekly maintenance program I'd developed. The company wasn't planning any major upgrades of hardware or software, so I had learned all I could. I was restless without challenges.

The third issue was the weather in Melbourne. I had never come to terms with waking on a winter's morning and hearing the wind and rain, knowing that I'd have to face umbrellas that blew inside out. Mum and Dad had moved to Stradbroke Island by then, and I had weekly reports of the glorious, blue-skied winters in Queensland.

I began searching the Situations Vacant columns in the classified sections of Brisbane newspapers, as well as checking some online employment websites. I discovered a position that suited me in a motor dealer group. The job was in the administration department. It looked like it was a busy position with varied duties. I hoped it might also entail some work with the computer system. I applied and was asked to attend an interview.

I took a day off work and caught an early flight, arriving late morning. My interview wasn't until three-thirty in the afternoon, but I wanted to get there with plenty of time to spare. During the flight I leaned my head back on the seat and closed my eyes, trying to visualise the interview. I had problems with that situation and felt it helpful to practice some 'scripts' in my head.

After leaving the terminal I took a cab to the Queen Street Mall and walked in and out of several shops until I found a shop assistant I felt I could communicate with. I told her the situation and the look I wanted to achieve. She brought me several outfits and watched as I walked around in each one. She was competent and capable, telling me honestly what worked and what didn't. We settled on a modern, dark pantsuit in a wool blend with a white cotton shirt. She told me of a pair of shoes two shops down that would look good and even rang the shop to see if they had my size. A salesperson from that store brought them to me so I could try them with the outfit. Perfect.

I made my purchases and then my amazing shop attendant rang a friend at a cosmetic counter in one of the major department stores. She wrote down the girl's name and sent me on my way. I was so grateful to her that my throat was constricting. I couldn't say thank you properly.

In no time my face was made-up to match my new corporate look. I had lunch, looked around some more and then caught a cab to the dealership. I arrived early but was taken in to the interview immediatcly.

The managing-director had the face of a comedian. His fair skinned was freckled and had deep lines where it creased from smiling. His mouth was wide and its angles indicated humour. There wasn't much hair on his scalp and what there was seemed to have a reddish tint. The irises of his eyes were so faded it was hard to tell if they were actually blue, as you would guess. He was brash and loud, but was also a straight-talker, which was the best I could have hoped for. I remembered my scripts and even relaxed a bit, which meant I was able to give a good account of myself.

"We're a bit of a mess, you see," he said. "We've grown quickly and our systems haven't. We need organising."

"Well," I laughed. "If it's organising you need then I'm your girl!"

He made an offer of salary that I knew was the minimum wage. It would mean a significant drop in income. I politely declined, giving my reasons. He laughed. "That was a test of your mettle, really. What were you hoping for?" I told him. He whistled and offered less, but with the use of a company car. We shook hands.

"When can you start?" I told him I had to give two weeks' notice and he nodded slowly. "Then you'll have to move your stuff up here and get settled."

"No, everything I own can be checked in as luggage in the hold."

"Yeah? Gee, what a girl. My wife can't even go away for the weekend with only that much."

We set a starting date and I left, still with enough time to see some rental properties with an agent. One of these was more than suitable - I fell in love with it immediately. The only problem was that it was also on the market and could be short-term. I signed a month-by-month lease.

I was shocked by my employer's reaction when I resigned. He became quite distressed. He offered more money and benefits, but eventually realised it was fruitless. I spent the remaining time there making sure I'd leave everything in excellent condition. On my last day my employer handed me a cheque for five thousand dollars out of his own personal bank account, making me promise to come back if things didn't work out 'up North'.

The townhouse I had rented exceeded my expectations. It was just perfect. There was only one problem, and that was a huge fluorescent light in the kitchen which was the only form of lighting in the room. When I first turned it on it made me feel sick, and I turned the switch off hurriedly, placing a piece of tape across it so I wouldn't turn it on by accident. I rang the agent and gained permission to change it at my own expense.

I visited a lighting shop and selected a single light-fitting which had a row of three adjustable spotlights that could be pointed where needed. Then I tried to hire an electrician on short notice. On the twelfth call I lucked out. He could come at four-thirty that day.

I spent that afternoon making a huge batch of lasagne. The plan was that I'd divide it into single portions and freeze it for my dinners. It was cooling on the sink when the electrician arrived.

He was a solid-looking man with a pleasant face and strong arms. Tufts of hair sprouted up from beneath the singlet under his navy work shirt and he was wearing shorts, long socks and running shoes. As he walked into the kitchen, he sniffed the air and saw the lasagne. "God, that smells like heaven," he said, rubbing his belly.

He started a stream of conversation that lasted the whole of the time it took to change the light fitting over. He'd just begun his own business; his marriage had failed so it was a good time for a change. His wife had always been against him leaving the security of a position with weekly wages, and without her he had the freedom to pursue his dream. They didn't have children, so it was easy.

He climbed down the ladder and flicked a switch in the circuit box. "Voila!" he said as the kitchen was bathed in a gentle light. He climbed back up the ladder and pointed the globes to where the light was needed most. It was done.

He looked at the lasagne again. "Gee, I love a good lasagne and yours looks bloody fantastic." He looked at me closely.

"Yes, it's a good recipe."

He was still looking at me as though expecting something. "Hey, I just had a really good idea. How about I knock thirty dollars off your bill and you share your lasagne with me. I haven't had much home cooking lately."

"Oh, I see. I guess that's okay."

"I'll just pack up my gear and have a wash. Can I use your bathroom?"

The townhouse was rented to me furnished, so I had a small dining table in the living area. I put out knives and forks with some folded paper towels in lieu of napkins. I poured a glass of water for each of us. I heard him coming back in.

He looked at the table and said, "We need some red wine. I'll be back in a few minutes." True to his word he was back quickly with a bottle of Shiraz. I'm not an early eater, so it felt weird, eating at six-fifteen.

He finished his serving quickly so I took his plate and served more. Eventually he pushed his chair back and patted his stomach. "That was bloody good! Thanks so much." I cleared our plates away and got some cash out of my purse.

"Hey, I've got another idea. How about we forget the bill altogether and you come out to dinner with me tomorrow night."

I frowned. What did this mean? He didn't want me to pay anything. He wanted to take me to dinner.

"Oh, like a date?"

He laughed. "Yes, you funny little thing. I think you are nice and I want to take you out on a date."

I thought about this for a moment.

"Where would we go?"

"Oh, I dunno. Somewhere nice. I'll call and let you know tomorrow."

He rang as promised to say we would go to a restaurant at the top of Mount Coot-tha. I looked up the website and saw pictures of the dining room. I always did better if I knew what to expect. I also checked out the menu. Now I needed a nice outfit.

The evening went well. He talked a lot about his plans for the business, and in my mind I could see what he needed to do. I offered suggestions that made him quite excited.

I took a pen and notebook out of my handbag and made some flowcharts. I also made a list of what computer and small business software he should invest in. His expression was quite comical. Obviously he had no idea.

"I'd pay you, you know. To set it all up in your spare time."

I shook my head. "Sorry but I've got too much happening at the moment. Lots of people could do this."

"Well okay, but perhaps you'd let me take you out again and I could pick your brains some more." I agreed to that.

This developing relationship was seductive in two ways. He was a big and capable man, who made me feel safe. He was gentle, kind and affectionate. He wasn't hard to be with. He had no hidden agendas.

I was also seduced by the fact he needed me. To be quite honest I was just itching to help him set the business up. It was good to put my skills to use when they were needed so badly. I could see clearly how the business model should look, and he just didn't have that vision.

Before I knew it, I was David's wife.

He didn't seem to mind that I needed time to myself. We ended up buying my much-loved townhouse, and one of the bedrooms became my bolt-hole. When I needed to, I would shut the door and write for hours. I guess that's why the relationship lasted as long as it did.

The business flourished and soon he needed a full-time office person and new premises. He wanted me to resign my position and work for him, but I refused. I enjoyed my work and the independence it provided.

When I became a mother, the Boss set me up with a laptop so I could work from home until Michael started kindergarten.

Eventually, of course, life became busier and more crowded. We moved to a bigger house and rented the townhouse out. Michael started to bring friends home after school and on weekends. David's business continued to grow, and he had to employ more and more electricians. He began to move and talk like an important man.

There were times we had to socialise for the good of the business. This became more frequent as time went by. Gradually I began to withdraw into myself.

Then the criticism began. Why couldn't I be like the

other wives? They dressed prettily and went shopping in groups. They played golf and tennis. They got their hair done weekly and had manicures and pedicures. Why did I insist on working for the motor group? I didn't need to. It was demeaning and it looked bad. It looked like I had to help him support the family. I just didn't fit in.

One day, during one of these attacks, I decided to try to inject some humour. "But I'm a great person to call on if you get a bad computer virus."

He looked at me with a face like a thundercloud. "I can pay people to do that now. I don't need you to do those things. I just need you to be a normal wife."

Inadvertently he had gone straight to the heart of the matter. He didn't need me anymore. He needed someone else now. I felt my heart turn to ice.

I shrank into myself and my soul began to wither. My writing suffered. I realised that his unconditional love had now become conditional on me acting as he wished.

I needed to get away from the awful man that David had become.

Then I met Christine.


I was thinking about this as I drove into Winton. My

research had unearthed some interesting facts. It was originally named Pelican Waterhole. "Once a Jolly Swagman" was first performed by Banjo Patterson in a Winton Hotel.

There were several pubs in town, and as I drove through I checked them out. I had already heard about the North Gregory Hotel. It was a local attraction and that's not the sort of place I wanted to be. The Tattersall's Hotel looked good, but I was too early for lunches so I went on to visit the local tourist bureau.

I could see the Dinosaur Trail. The Waltzing Matilda Centre was apparently a must. I could visit the actual Pelican Waterhole that the town was originally named after. I could go on an opal walk. I felt my mouth turning down. I just wasn't in the mood.

I drove out to the Pelican Waterhole and took a snapshot of the strange statue. There was an Asian couple there who asked if I could take their photograph standing in front of it. They told me they were on their honeymoon and really enjoying their outback adventure.

It was ten-thirty. I hit the Tattersall's Hotel.


I had come to believe that the barmaids in the outback were

all cloned from an original somewhere. This woman had her name displayed on a tag: Marge. She was big and buxom with blonde/grey hair pulled sharply from her face. Oddly she was wearing fake diamond earrings that hung from her lobes in strands.

The bar was quiet and cool. I sat and asked her about sandwiches and a stubby of light beer.

"Sure, dear. What would you like in your sandwiches?"

I asked for brown bread, no butter or margarine, and just an assortment of whatever they had.

"No butter?"

"No thanks."

"Or margarine?"

"No."

"Oh, okay. I'll let the kitchen know."

She placed the order and produced a stubby of light beer.

"Can't eat butter?"

"No, I get upset stomachs really easily. Anything high in fat sets it off."

"From the city are you?"

"Yes."

"Seems that you city folk have delicate constitutions."

"Must be all the stress."

"Well, we have stress here you know. Probably the same sort. Usually caused by men!" She thumped the bar and roared with laughter.

I joined in. "You can say that again."

"You're here alone? Divorced are you?"

"Yes. I've been married twice and divorced twice."

"Sounds like a lot of trouble to go through. Mine just shot through one day."

"Oh, I'm sorry to hear that."

"Nah, it was the best day of my life." She brushed a fly away from her nose. "He was a bastard. Were yours bastards?"

"Well, I guess that depends on what you mean by bastard. I didn't like the second one much in the end."

"Did they whack you and the kids?"

"No."

"Mine did…"

# MARGE'S STORY

"You wouldn't believe this, would ya? I was once a Sydney city girl. Oooh, I was pretty, too. Slim and pretty. 'Ave a look at this!" She took a tattered photograph from a man's style wallet she had in her pocket.

I looked and saw she was right. How did this pretty and slender girl end up being this overblown and unattractive woman? I couldn't think of a thing to say, so I handed the photograph back with a weak smile.

"It could only be a man, eh? Only a man could cause so much shit in a woman's life." She blew her cheeks out and swatted a fly that was finding something interesting in her hair.

"I was sharing a flat with a girl from work. We were both secretaries in the public service and we were having a fat time, I can tell ya. There were so many nice men wanderin' in and out of our flat it felt like we 'ad one of those revolving doors, ya know?" She gave me a lusty wink.

"Anyways, one day me flatmate's brother rolled into town from out this way. God that man was a dream. Turned into a nightmare, but right then and there he was drop-dead gorgeous. Tall and handsome and with muscles like you wouldn't believe. We took one look at each other and that was that. We was married in a few weeks and I quit me job and came out 'ere with him." She looked out the windows into the dusty street and sighed.

"I 'ad a bun in the oven in no time, of course. The way we were at each other, it's a wonder it wasn't quads or somthin'. We only 'ad a small room to rent and soon there was three of us. He didn't take well to being a dad."

She paused, lost in her own thoughts. I could tell she was back there, living in that room.

"He started working out of town more and more, takin' on shearing and fencing. He'd roll back into town on Friday night all tired and dusty. Saturday night was drinkin' night with his mates. On Sundays we'd sleep in, well as much as the bub would let us, and then he'd go orf again, into the bush.

"I had the second bub within fourteen months of the first. It was a real crier, that one. Drove me nuts. Frank couldn't stand it even for a few minutes. He'd stay out later on Saturday nights and come home really rotten. When the bub cried he'd get all nasty and start hitting me.

"Me Mum was still back in the suburbs of Sydney and I went and stayed with her for a bit. I tried to tell 'er wot was goin' on but she just told me that my place was with me 'usband and just packed me off back to 'ere.

"Soon I 'ad three kiddies under three years old. We were still in that room, and it was hell. Frank got worse and worse and every Saturday night I was turned into a punchin' bag. Ended up I would pack me and the kids up and we'd go and sleep in a park and only go home when I figured he was asleep."

I shook my head in sympathy. I'd heard stories like this before, but never from the person who'd lived through it. I noticed some tears forming in her eyes and knew there was worse to come.

"I lost the oldest one, me gorgeous Sally. Ended up she'd had a kidney problem since she was born and we dinna know. She died suddenly like, and I went to pieces. Me landlady helped out a lot - started taking the other two for a few hours here and there. Frank left straight after the funeral and I didn't see him for a month.

"Rumour had it that he'd taken up with some woman in another town. I 'ad no money and had to ask me Mum for some. She sent a bit, but not enough. I started workin' 'ere at the pub and paid me landlady to look after the kids."

She walked towards a customer, greeting them cheerily while wiping tears from her cheeks.

"He'd come back every now and again, me Frank. Sometimes I'd find me wages missing from me purse when he'd gone again. I only asked 'im once about it and got whacked for me trouble. From then on I didn't say anythin', I'd just work overtime to make up for it."

"So, you never told him to go away? That you wanted a divorce?"

She snorted. "Times were different back then. It just wasn't that easy. And ya know...I still loved him, even though he was such a bastard. He never told me when he'd be going or when he'd be back. He just wandered in and out whenever 'e wanted somethin', ya know?"

I shook my head. I didn't know. I couldn't comprehend such a life.

"Anyways, I didn't see him for a couple of months and then he rolled back into town and said he'd decided to live with this other woman permanent like, and that he was divorcing me. It seemed such a joke, him leavin' me after all I'd put up with. I lost it then. I hit 'im with a saucepan. He took off and that's the last I ever saw of 'im. I was sad back then, but now I see it was the best thing that 'appened to me."

"But you stayed here? Didn't go back to Sydney?"

"Oh, I took time off and went to see me Mum, but somehow I didn't belong there anymore. The people here were real good to me, ya know? They sorta watched over me without making a fuss of it. I'd find a box of veggies at my door, or a parcel of meat. Me boss and his wife 'ere have been real good to me. Always made sure I never went without. And me customers…you know I've been serving the same people 'ere for thirty-five years. They're like family. If a stranger rolls into the bar and gives me trouble, let me tell ya, there's an army waitin' to defend me. I can't think of a single reason to leave 'ere, ya know?"

I nodded. The best family are sometimes the people you choose, not the ones you're landed with.

"So you never remarried?"

"Gawd no! Go through that again? Anyways, a divorcee with two kids isn't too attractive to blokes around 'ere. Oh, I've spent some time with one or two of them but it never worked out. I put all my time and energy into my kids. It's not their fault their father was a dribblin' arsehole. I've raised 'em good and strong and I'm proud of that."

"I guess he never paid any support, either?"

"Nah, but I never chased 'im for it either. Seemed easier to just 'ave him out of our lives. I could make all the decisions that way - bring 'em up right."

"So they live here in town?"

"Took off as soon as they could. Me son is in the mines in WA. Me daughter is in Sydney, doing Design at Uni. She works part time to support 'erself and shares a house with a whole lotta other students. Do you know what she works as, part time?"

I shook my head.

"She works in a bar!" She let out a roar of laughter. "Must've got it from her Mum. Earns good money, but. One of those fancy places. Good on 'er, I say. The only trouble is, I don't hardly see 'em any more. They never bring their friends to meet me or anything. Do you think they're ashamed of me or somethin'?"

Poor woman. She'd struggled and fought to bring up her children, giving them every opportunity to grow, unencumbered by the negatives of their lives. I hoped they weren't ashamed of her, otherwise she'd failed to make them good human beings.

"No, I'm sure they're not ashamed at all. How could they be? They've just got busy lives and that's the way it should be. Clearly you've raised them to believe that they don't owe you anything, that they don't have to hang around here to look after you. That's a wonderful gift you've given them."

Her face cracked into a smile. "Yeah, you're right. That's it, isn't it? You've just made me feel a whole lot better." Her faced suddenly looked more youthful, and as she wiped the bar she let out a sigh that sounded like it had been a long time coming.

Seeing a customer walking through the door she said. "Hey Georgie-Porgy. How are you, you gorgeous hunk of a man? The usual?"

# CHAPTER TEN

North of Winton I was tearing along the road when I nearly ran into a herd of cattle. I had been fiddling with the stereo system and had taken my eyes off the road for a few seconds and found myself having to brake hard to avoid a nasty and messy collision. A road train travelling in the opposite direction had also pulled up.

The driver jumped down from his cab and started waving at the cattle with his hat. It didn't seem to help much. I got out and tried to help him. We ended up laughing at our efforts.

"I saw you had to stop mighty quick. You can't take your eyes of the road here, 'cause it's unfenced."

I looked around and saw it was true. The highway was part of the paddock.

"That must cause you problems if you drive through a lot."

"Yeah, I've collected a few with my bull bar from time to time. It would be different for you, though. You'd mess up the front end of that nice little car of yours. Tom's the name."

"Hi Tom. I'm Janine." I became aware of how relaxed I was with this total stranger.

"Where're you headed?"

"Cloncurry."

"Ah, not far then."

"No, I've come from Longreach. I've still got a few hours."

"Yeah, the road's pretty good, if you don't take your eyes off it, that is."

He wiped his forehead and stared off into the distance.

"Where're you from?"

"Brisbane."

"Ah nice. I've never been there but I heard it's good."

"Where are you from?"

"Darwin."

"Oh, I'll be there in a few days."

"Really? We should get together for a drink to laugh about our cattle handling efforts."

He went back to his truck and came back with a mobile. "Give me your number."

I recited it and he smiled in satisfaction. "I'll take you for a beer somewhere, eh?"

"Great."

We looked around to see that the cattle had miraculously wandered back into the scrub.

"Well, I'd better get going. Nice to meet you Tom."

"Likewise. See you in Darwin."

The photographs I'd taken of the people who had told me their stories were technically imperfect, but good nonetheless. The latest one, Marge the barmaid, was the best so far in terms of light and depth. My favourite was Jenny, the aboriginal woman. What an interesting face! I not only saved them to the laptop but sent them to cloud storage where I kept all my manuscripts in case of computer failure.

Marge still had tears running down her face from the telling of her story when she signed my piece of paper. I filed it with the other one in the back of my notebook. I thought about the human capacity for suffering and how, sometimes, we don't duck and weave enough to avoid it. We stay in situations and relationships far longer than we should in the hopes of what? Things will get better? They rarely do. We just suffer.

My suffering, in the dying stages of my marriage to David, was cut short by a remark from Chris. I was sitting at my desk, designing a new form for customer loan vehicles. When the phone rang, I reached out and lifted the receiver, still looking at my screen.

"Hi, honeybunch. It's me!"

My heart lifted. "Hey, you! What are you up to?"

"I've just delivered a car and I'm on my way back to work. I might stop off somewhere for lunch. Do you want to meet me?"

I looked at my watch. "Yeah, I can leave in a few minutes. It's a beautiful day. How about a park or something?"

Chris bought sandwiches and juice and I met her in the park at Breakfast Creek. We sat under a tree near the wedding gazebo and watched the creek flow by. Beyond that was Kingsford Smith Drive and all its traffic. I sighed with pleasure.

"You look happy today," said Chris.

"I am now I'm with you."

"How was David this morning?" Chris knew how bad things were at home.

"His usual, critical self."

"You keep saying it's over, but you don't leave him.

Why is that?"

I shrugged. "I fully intend to. I guess I'm just waiting for the right time. Michael has exams coming up, and then it's his birthday."

"Then it's Christmas, then Easter......"

I laughed. "Yes, I know."

Chris frowned. "I've got something to say to you."

"Yes?"

"I don't want to share you with them anymore. I want us to be together properly. I want you to leave David and live with me."

With this statement, her bottom lip had started to wobble and her deep blue eyes were moist. She was adorable. I leaned over and kissed that lip.

"Consider it done," I said.

"What did you just say?" His face was crimson and he was bellowing at me.

"You heard. I don't need to repeat it."

David had met Chris often and I could tell he was very attracted to her. She had spent time at our house, sometimes staying the night. I had set up a mattress on the floor of my writing room for her to sleep on, and also for me on those nights when sharing a bed with David had become intolerable.

We would all say goodnight and Chris would disappear into the writing room, but leave the door ajar. As soon as David began snoring, I'd creep in there and we'd giggle and snuggle up together, as happy and playful as two puppies in a basket.

David was breathing heavily. "You mean you're going to live with Chris *as her lover?*" I nodded.

"Bullshit! I won't have it! I won't allow it!" I didn't dignify this absurd statement with a reply.

"Don't think you're taking Michael! I won't let him be raised by a couple of dykes. I don't even want him visiting you there on weekends. In fact, don't even call either of us."

I began putting some books in a box.

"I always knew there was something wrong with you. Now I know for sure."

I reached over for another box to put the rejected books in to.

"Don't think you'll get a cent out of me, either." That was also a ridiculous statement. I was entitled to half of our assets. The thing was, I didn't want or need them. I wasn't going to enter into a protracted and exhausting fight with David. It just wasn't worth it.

I could tell my silence was enraging him further.

"You know, you're just an emotionless bitch!" Now he was roaring at me. "You always have been. I've told you I'm taking your son away and that you'll get no money, but still you just keep packing. I used to think you were a calm person but now I now there's just nothing there behind that facade. You're a bloody monster and you should have been drowned at birth."

That did hurt. It felt like I'd been kicked in the stomach.

"Alright, just piss off then. I'm going to pick Michael up from football practice. I want you gone by the time we get back.

I was.

As I typed up the details of Madge's story, I thought about how much better off she would have been if she had just left her husband as soon as his true nature was revealed. You can't teach an old dog new tricks. I finished and filed the document and also sent a copy of it, and the other stories, to the cloud. This was becoming valuable work.

The salt water pool was delightful, and I swam for an hour. I washed clothes and hung them to dry, knowing the hot, dry climate would make this easy. The heat was still shimmering in the distance, and I was glad to get back to my air-conditioned room.

There were several tourist brochures on the stand next to the television. I flicked through them, noting John Flynn Place and an interesting cemetery. John Flynn was the founder of the Royal Flying Doctor Service, and a museum and art gallery was built in his honour. The cemetery is interesting due to the graves of the Afghan and Chinese workers who were buried there.

I also read about the ill-fated exploration of the area by Burke and Wills as well as the importance of copper in the history of the town. I got bored and decided to head somewhere for a drink.

This is what I wrote that night when I came back to my room:

*I never found out John Three's real name. He was in the bar when I arrived at the hotel, with a beer in one hand and a fresh one by his elbow. He was a big, brutish looking man with a heavy brow and slack mouth. As I walked in he looked me up and down. I bought a beer and took it to a table that was in full view of his wolfish gaze.*

*He looked affluent in beige chinos and a white linen shirt. His boots, which looked like they were made by R.M. Williams, had a high shine. I saw him motion to the barman and heard him say in a loud voice, "Who's the filly?" The barman looked in my direction and said something I couldn't hear. I looked in another direction, but could feel his lascivious gaze on me the whole time.*

*Finally I rose and took my drink over to him. "Do you have a room here?" I asked. He nodded.*

*"I'm three hundred dollars for an hour."*

*There was silence for a moment. His face lost all expression, then came back to life.*

*"You don't look like one of those hooker girls."*

*"I'm not. But that's my price. We could go right now."*

*He finished his beer in one long draw, and I followed him up the staircase. I thought he might be a wealthy grazier, in town for a few days on business. His loud voice reminded me of my father, whose hearing was damaged by too many hours on agricultural machinery.*

*He was rough, bordering on violent. Neither of us was carrying condoms, and I found I didn't care whether he used one or not. I just wanted it hard and fast with an edge of brutality, and that is why I chose him. It was over quickly. He rolled on to his back and closed his eyes. "You can go now."*

*I dressed quickly and left.*

I have just opened *We of the Never Never* again and

found my place:

*"For a moment we waited, spell-bound in the brilliant sunshine; then the dogs running down to the water's edge, the gallahs and cockatoos rose with gorgeous sunrise effect: a floating gray-and-pink cloud, backed by sunlit flashing white. Direct to the forest trees they floated and, settling there in their myriads, as by a miracle the gaunt, gnarled old giants of the bush all over blossomed with garlands of grey, and pink, and white, and gold."*

I will let Jeannie Gunn soothe me to sleep.

I passed through an interesting region called the Ayrshire Hills. These strange formations looked out of place in this landscape and I found them fascinating. I took some time photographing them.

When I finished I took a moment to look up at the sky. It was clear and light and so incredibly high that it seemed like I was nearly looking right into the heavens. The only sound I could hear was my breathing. It felt like being in a vacuum and I loved the quality of the silence. It soothed me.

After this, the road became more undulating and it seemed like grasslands had taken the place of the mulga. It was almost pleasant. The road was still good, although it had been patched many times. Road trains were plentiful, and each time I passed one I thought of Tom. It seemed I'd have a friend in Darwin.

I rolled into Cloncurry late in the afternoon, before the kangaroos would become a problem. I prayed my luck would stay with me with a place to rest my head. There was a highly rated Inn/hotel which boasted a guest laundry and salt-water pool and my hopes were high that I could stay there.

I walked into the reception area and was greeted by a young girl. I asked if she had a room available. She stared in to a book for a while. "Nah, all taken, sorry."

"Damn. I was really hoping to stay here. There isn't any sort of room at all, or the chance of a cancellation?"

"How long're staying?"

"I think it's just overnight."

"Nah.....not unless you want to pay extra for an Executive Room."

I looked at her with raised eyebrows. "So you do have a room of a sort available."

"Yeah, but it's an Executive, like I said."

"How much extra is it?"

"Twenny bucks."

"How much is a standard room."

"$160."

"So this is only $180?"

"Yeah, but people don't like paying the extra."

I was almost out of patience.

"I'll take it, thanks."

"Are you sure?"

"Yes. Have you worked here long?"

"This is my third day."

"I see. Have you been in hospitality long?"

"Huh?"

"Never mind. Here's my credit card."

# CHAPTER ELEVEN

The Matilda Highway had become a friend to me, and I felt sad to be leaving its benign presence.

After checking out, I drove to a service station and gave the SUV a good going over. I checked the tyre pressure, oil and water, cleaned the windscreen and tossed out some rubbish that had accumulated.

I took some photographs of the cemetery, noting how the Afghan graves all faced Mecca. I did a quick tour of the John Flynn Centre, all three floors, and then drove out of town. It was already very hot at nine o'clock in the morning.

When copper became big business in the region, Mount Isa was set up as an administrative centre. It was a drive of only one and a half hours or so along a good road which ran between large hills. I had the radio tuned to ABC Radio National, but became annoyed at the chatter and switched to CD. It was old style Jazz, early Thelonious Monk. His keyboard improvisations were the perfect accompaniment to the open road.

There were many hills and a couple of interesting places on the way: the Burke and Wills memorial, and the Mary Kathleen copper mine. I stopped at the memorial and took a photograph of the squat, rocky obelisk, finding it funny that some chains had been erected around it, supported by bent white metal poles. The chains were only half a metre from the ground and I wondered what they were meant to keep out. Perhaps they were only meant for decoration.

I was in the Gulf Country, which sounded very exciting. I wondered about the early explorers of this region, including Burke and Wills. How on earth did they survive in this harsh environment?

Mount Isa has been described as the "Oasis of the Outback", and it certainly looked like one as I drove in to it. It felt affluent, mostly due to the huge Mount Isa Mine. Copper, silver and zinc were found to be plentiful in the area, and the whole community has reaped the benefits that mining these minerals created.

I drove around for a while and got a feel for the place. I saw several haulage trucks and thought about Andrew

Potter and how he'd made his fortune here.

I wasn't interested in visiting any mining museums, so after buying a sandwich at a cafe, I drove out the other side of town.

I didn't find anything enjoyable or adventurous about the Barkly Highway which stretches from Mount Isa to Tennant Creek. It was desolate and uninteresting.

After nearly six hours I stopped at Barkly Homestead for petrol and decided to stay the night. I was dispirited and edgy. I had driven a long way since leaving Brisbane and now felt like I'd run out of steam. The Homestead offered motel rooms surrounded by a large shady veranda. My room had a queen bed and two singles and also a clean and modern bathroom. I threw my gear onto one of the single beds and splashed cold water on my gritty face. I stripped down to underwear and lay on the big bed with a sigh. I looked at the ceiling for a while and then took out my book.

I must have dozed for more than an hour and woke disoriented, with tears running down my face. I had been dreaming about trying to find Chris. I'd try to press numbers on my mobile to call her, but the screen would turn blank. I'd try to drive to her but my car wouldn't start.

I was crying with frustration.

The room had darkened while I was asleep and that matched my gloomy mood. I brushed the tears from my face and lay there trying to remember every detail of the dream. It had brought Chris back into close focus, whereas when awake I had tried to block her from my mind.

In the dream she was at our townhouse and I was trying to get home to her. Something had upset me badly and I needed her to soothe me and help me make sense of it. That's what she did for me. She decoded the mysteries of life. There was so much I just couldn't understand of the world, especially when it came to people. She would be able to explain it to me in a way that ripped off the opaque veils of mystery and left the substance that I could deal with. Life was very hard without her. I found it peaceful to be alone, but I knew that when it came to Chris, I could find a deeper, more satisfying peace. My soul was at rest. During that time we lived together, I wrote beautiful passages of prose, the words spilling from my mind. She did that for me, and without her I was stressed and inconsolable.

I don't think we ever had an argument. We each had our individual talents and made sure the other person had room to use and develop them. There were a few tense moments when we first moved in together, though.

Being the organised one of the two of us, I found us somewhere to live and then made it habitable for us. She understood that I needed time alone between leaving David and being with her and she respected it.

We could not have lived in her flat; neither of us liked it. I found us a townhouse to rent which was brand new and had a balcony that faced north-east. It had three bedrooms and two bathrooms.

I moved in first and began taking care of all the necessary arrangements. I had to find an electrician to replace the fluorescent lights, a fact I found amusing. I then purchased furniture and kitchen items, electrical appliances and outdoor furniture. Our bed was a top of the range king size. My writing desk was beautiful, and I bought a new, very comfortable office chair to go with it. By the time I finished, the townhouse looked amazing in the minimalist style I loved.

I arranged a telephone connection, then ADSL broadband. Then I set up a wireless network. I filled the cupboards and refrigerator with food. Chris was popping in and out a lot throughout this time. After two weeks, on a weekend, she moved all her boxes over to the new place.

I have never seen a worse pile of horrendous junk in all my life, and she planned to bring it in to this lovely new pristine environment of ours. I stopped her at the door and suggested we go through it all in the garage. We arranged two piles, one of things she quickly agreed she didn't need and would donate to charity. The other was for the things she felt she couldn't live without. We put those things back into a box and put that in the garage cupboard. There it remained, mostly forgotten.

The near-argument came the day after she moved in. She realized that I had spent a great deal of money setting the house up and wanted to talk about it.

"I'm really broke, I'm sorry. Money just disappears and I can never save. I must owe you a lot for all of this."

"No, money isn't a problem. I can get it any time."

She frowned. "What do you mean?"

"If I need money I can get it easily. I just spend a week or two doing short term buying/selling on the stock exchange."

"Huh?"

"I have a trading account and I select some shares that I know will go up in value—"

"How do you know that?"

"What?"

"That they'll go up in value?"

"I don't know. I just look at the company history and

the recent share fluctuations and it's like my brain just computes it without me really knowing how."

"And you're always right?"

"No, not always, but most of the time.

"So you could just keep doing this and make millions?"

"Well, I never thought of it that way, but I guess so."

"Then why don't you?"

I frowned. "Because I have enough money."

She stared at me for a moment.

"So you're telling me that you could just do this every day and make tons of money, but you just don't because you don't need it?"

"Yes, that's right."

"We could give up work and travel the world!"

"We can work and still travel in our holidays. It's better for us. Gives structure to our lives."

This discussion went on for half an hour and nearly became an argument. To appease her I promised to do some trading and set up a fund of one hundred thousand dollars for fun money. We called it our slush fund, and I always kept it topped up.

Other than that we lived in a state of bliss. She never criticised me and went out of her way to make me comfortable in any social situation we found ourselves in.

She warned me if anyone was going to drop in for a visit. If we entertained it was usually just one or two people, and she would take time to tell me about the people invited, their personality traits and habits. If we were going out, she would help me select items from my wardrobe. I began to look better 'put together'. Even my work wardrobe improved.

My life was peaceful and harmonious, and I shared it with the best and most beautiful person in the world.

It couldn't last, of course.

I was shaken out of these thoughts by the shrilling of my mobile. It was the Boss.

"Hey Janine. Where are you?"

"Hi. I'm at a place called Barkly Homestead between Mount Isa and Tenant Creek."

"Are you okay?"

"Yeah, I'm okay. I'm feeling a bit lonely tonight, but it's all good really. I'm just about to go and see what there is here. I'll have some dinner. How are things there?"

"Oh, okay. We all miss you."

"That's nice. I miss you too." That was one of the little lies I'd learned to say from time to time. It made people feel better.

"So you're still heading for Broome?"

"Yes, that's the plan."

"Still okay for money?"

"Yes, I'm good, thanks."

"Okay then. I'll let you go and explore around the place. Stay safe, eh?"

"I will. Thanks for the call."

I stretched my limbs and pulled on my jeans and t-shirt. I walked along the veranda and as I came to the end of it I saw the sky. What a show! The stars were brilliant and plentiful. I don't think I'd ever seen such a bright, starry night. The newish crescent moon was sitting low in the western sky, just about to disappear for the night. I stood in awe for a long time.

The homestead was busy. It seemed to be a popular stop off point for travellers, and there were road trains, four-wheel drives, and caravans strewn all over the grounds. Some people were pitching tents on grassed areas, while others were parking their caravans on powered sites. I walked around in the gentle evening air, nodding to people who said hello, noting the various number plates which hinted at the origin of the vehicles and the people in them.

Finally I arrived back at the main building. There were

delicious smells coming from the Bar and Grill, and I went inside.

This was beef country, and I was hungry. I ordered a fillet steak with salad and fries. It arrived quickly, and I washed it down with a cold beer. The steak was cooked to perfection and cut like butter. I was impressed.

I wasn't in the mood for either conversation or company. I went back to my room. I played solitaire on my laptop for hours until my eyelids began drooping. I fell into bed.

# CHAPTER TWELVE

Nothing was quite working right for me in terms of how far to travel each day. I knew there was some boring driving ahead, so I decided to skip Tenant Creek and head straight for Daly Waters. It is a drive of seven hours or so.

I bypassed Camooweal and kept heading west. Soon I came to a sign that said "Welcome to Nature Territory, the Northern Territory of Australia". I had just left Queensland after days of driving. Had I been in parts of Europe I would have passed through several small countries by now.

The speed limit rose to 130kph. That's what I'd been doing anyway. I took it up to 145. After a stretch of deteriorating road, it came good again.

I was thoroughly sick of red dust. The t-shirts I'd bought in Roma were originally white. Now, however hard I scrubbed them, they had a residual red tint. I could taste the dust in my mouth and took frequent sips of water to try to be rid of it.

I wasn't getting any good photographs of the desert like I'd hoped. I didn't even want to leave the car to attempt any. I just drove and drove.

My mood wasn't improved by my period arriving that morning. It wasn't the fact it had come, but noticing the nature of it. The flow was very light and the blood dark, just like the previous two periods I'd had. It made me wonder what was changing in my body. "Oh, God!" I thought. "Could it be the first signs of menopause?"

I was so shocked by this thought that I pulled off the road. How old was I? Forty-four? Yes, forty-five next birthday. I searched my brain for information about the 'change of life', but didn't really have any stored. I never thought about getting older. I still felt eighteen or nineteen. I still looked young. I recalled what Chris had said on the subject.

One morning, a few days after she moved into the townhouse with me, she went to use her hairdryer. It smoked and crackled and tripped the safety switch in the circuit box. She came up to the bathroom I used and asked to use mine.

"I don't own one."

"Naw, come on. I'm running late and need it urgently.

Hand it over."

"I'm serious. I don't own a hairdryer."

I saw her look at my hair. "What do you use to get your hair so nice?"

"Nothing. It just goes that way. I just use an afro comb on it."

"Bullshit!"

"Chris, I'm serious."

"What products do you use? She began opening the cupboards and drawers in my bathroom.

"None."

"You haven't got anything in here! What do you use on that gorgeous skin of yours?"

"Just Ponds like my mother used to use."

"Christ. You have hardly any wrinkles! Next you'll be telling me you don't do anything to make your brows look as great as they are."

I just looked at her.

"How long does it take you to do your hair and face every morning?"

I shrugged. "Ten minutes, including the shower."

"Ten minutes including your shower to look as stunning as you do. I want to see a photo of you when you were twenty."

I found one on my laptop and showed her. "Just as I suspected. You haven't aged a day." It sounded like an accusation.

I looked at the picture and found she was right. Nothing had changed at all.

"I think it's just as well your beauty routine is simple. I think that if it was any harder you just wouldn't bother. You're just not into cosmetics and hair products."

"True."

She looked at her watch and wailed. "What am I going to do to get this hair of mine styled?"

As I recalled this, a huge sadness came over me and it was worse than what I'd felt so far. I thought about menopause. I was still young. I wasn't ready to cross over into middle age. It just didn't make sense.

What did life hold for me from now on? I was alone and would probably stay so. I was finished with close relationships. There would be no one to look after me, to watch over me, to witness the history and events of the second half of my life. Would I eventually end up in some sort of nursing home, without anyone to visit me? Would I have to share a room with someone? I began to feel sick at the thought. One of my conditions of becoming pregnant was that I wouldn't have to share a room in the hospital with anyone when the baby came. Imagine, having to share personal space with strangers?

Suddenly I missed my mother with a ferocity that took me unawares. I could have asked her about menopause—found out what age she first noticed symptoms. She would have sat me down and spoken softly to me. What would she have said?

My mother. She was one of those rare, selfless, kind and giving people who deserve sainthood. I didn't see her get angry, not once in her life. She didn't growl, smack or criticise. My mother's method of parenting was to praise good behaviour and if we weren't behaving well, she would simply divert us to some other activity. It wasn't until I was a mother myself that I saw the cleverness in this method. I attempted to emulate it, with mixed success.

She was small and buxom with wide hips and thin hair. All her energy went into making sure my father, sister and I were 'well turned out', and there never seemed to be enough resources, either in time or money, to spend on herself. Her glasses were cheap 'magnifiers' from the chemist that she wore around her neck on a plastic chain. Often they would sit on the end of her nose so she could look down and read print if needed.

She didn't help my father on the farm, and this seemed to be due to some prior agreement. I don't think I even ever saw her in a paddock. All her time was spent caring for her family while all my father's time was spent running the farm. I'm sure he would have liked a son to help him, but had to be content with hiring help when necessary.

My mother baked delights that had us running home at the end of the day to see what the latest offerings were. These would be enjoyed with a glass of fresh milk before starting our homework. Her Sunday roasts were glorious, served with golden roast potatoes that were crisp on the outside and fluffy in the middle.

Where my father was a remote parent, Mum was the one available 24/7 for anything we might need. Where Dad was taciturn, Mum was effusive. Where Dad never displayed his affection physically, Mum always had open arms and loads of hugs and kisses. Where Dad seemed to take strange pleasure in drowning unwanted kittens and puppies, Mum would work hard to save a baby bird that had fallen from a nest.

As children, our birthday parties were miraculous. The party bags Mum put together to give out to our friends were spoken about for weeks. I now wonder at the time and energy she put into these events.

I think I puzzled her sometimes, but she didn't say anything. I'd just find her looking at me as though I were a hard clue in a crossword she was trying to figure out. I was different to the rest of them - I now know why - but she loved me all the same without reserve.

Dad's attitude toward Mum was hard to comprehend. It was a mixture of mild exasperation and borderline sarcasm. Did he think her a bit simple, perhaps? Did he see himself as superior to her? Sometimes she became flustered at his attitude, which seemed to make things worse.

She didn't drive a car often, but when she did it was with her whole body pushed forward, her nose only millimetres from the windscreen, her knuckles white on the steering wheel. She would drive painfully slowly, turning on the indicators where it wasn't necessary. I think Dad had, over the years, destroyed any confidence she may have once had in her abilities as a driver.

It was rare to find her sitting in a relaxed position. Sometimes she would pick up a magazine and drop into a chair by the range to do a crossword puzzle. As she got older, sometimes her head would start nodding and she'd jump awake when the magazine slid to the floor with a bang.

When my first marriage broke up, she said little but gave me extra hugs and knitted me two jumpers. We had already lost her by the time my second marriage dissolved.

Her lifetime of eating cakes, biscuits, and foods high in animal fats took their toll. Dad was active enough to fight their effect, and perhaps he also had better genes. Mum's family had a history of heart problems, with very few adults living past sixty-five. She passed away after several years of severe health problems, so it wasn't entirely unexpected. Nothing prepares you for that telephone call, however.

If Dad missed Mum after her death he never showed it. He simply made his own plans, free to live the way he wanted. He looked after himself adequately and had a routine which he was loathe to break.

Sometimes I wondered about his habit of using some of her favourite things: plates, cups and saucers, and so forth. I eventually came to the conclusion that it wasn't to preserve her memory, but rather because to throw them out would be a sinful waste.

Now that I needed her advice so badly, what could I imagine she would say? I guess her advice on menopause would be similar to the talk she gave me when I first found blood in my underpants. She would sit me down on my bed and clasp my hand between hers. She would talk about how wonderful nature was and how this was just a phase in my life leading to a whole new stage. She would talk about how every woman goes through it. Her eyes would be soft and blue with crinkles at the edges. Her voice would be gentle and a bit breathless. She would make me feel relieved and happy.

When Andrew talked about that moment on the ship when he felt his parents' love in the brilliance of the dawn, I immediately thought of my mother. It gave me hope that she's up there somewhere, still in her support-hose and sensible shoes, looking down on me and glowing with benign love. What I would give to know it was true!

I was shocked from these thoughts by encountering several road trains in quick succession. The last one threw up a stone that cracked my windscreen. Several kilometres on from there I felt the tell-tale wobbling in the steering caused by a flat tyre. I cursed and pulled over.

I knew how to change a tyre, but my memory was rather rusty. I looked in the glove compartment and saw there was no owner's manual. I retrieved the tools from the rear of the SUV and stood looking at the tyre.

A car pulled up behind mine. It was a large, white

four-wheel-drive with a man and woman inside. They were towing a smart-looking caravan.

The man leapt out with energy. "A flat tyre, eh? Want a hand?"

I smiled gratefully and passed him the wrench. He tackled the job with enthusiasm. After a few minutes, I found the woman at my elbow.

"It must be hard, travelling on your own. Don't you feel helpless?"

"No, I actually prefer it. Until I get a flat tyre, that is."

"Wow. I wish I was like you."

The man had the wheel off and was putting the spare in its place.

"Where are you headed today?" he asked.

"Daly Waters."

"That's where we're staying tonight."

I nodded.

"Perhaps you'll come and have a drink with us. Anne there is getting a bit tired of my company, I think. Isn't that right?"

She smiled weakly. "It would be nice to have a woman to talk to."

The man finished the job and wiped his hands on his shorts.

"I suppose you'll be in a cabin at the pub?"

I hadn't researched Daly Waters yet. I hadn't had internet access for a few days.

"Would that be my best option?"

"There's the Hi-Way Inn, but the pub has more history and character."

"Yes, I'll be there then."

"What's your name?"

"Janine Waldron."

"Hi Janine. I'm Jack and this is Anne. We'll see you there."

I waited until they pulled away then sat for a few minutes thinking. If I wanted to survive without Chris, I had to learn to befriend people. I had to swallow my horror of having to go and 'have drinks' with the likes of Jack and Anne. I would go there and be friendly. I would think about topics of conversation—have a list in my mind and raise them one by one. I would ask questions about their lives even though I wouldn't be remotely interested in the answers. I could do this. I really could.


Three kilometres from the Stuart Highway is the Daly Waters Historic Pub. Given the fact I'd cracked a windscreen and blew a tyre that day, I didn't really expect to have much luck securing accommodation without a reservation. I asked for the best they had and was given a free-standing cabin with two bedrooms. It wasn't five-star but it was clean and comfortable.

I took my tyre to the service station for repair, then came back, changed, and plunged in to the salt water pool. It was heaven.

I was sorting things in my room when there was a knock on the door.

"Yoo-hoo! It's only Jack. Are you ready for that drink yet?"

I wrapped a sarong around my speedos and walked to the screen door.

"Hi Jack. Just give me a few minutes. Where can I meet you?"

He pointed to a cabin a few doors down. "Anne was sick to death of the caravan, so we got a room. See you soon!"

I walked down to the pub and bought some stubbies and crisps. When I got to their cabin, I could see Jack and Anne through the screen door. They looked like characters from a still life painting, waiting for me to animate them. I called out, and they told me to just walk in.

"I bought two sorts of beer, Jack. I owed you a drink for helping me out today."

"It was nothing. Everyone helps each other in the outback."

Jack settled back in his chair and began talking. With a sinking stomach I realised what sort of man he was. He had lots and lots of stories. He had told them often, to anyone who would listen. He thought they were interesting and amusing, but they weren't. They were just boring.

A couple of times I tried to talk to Anne, but Jack was adept at stealing the conversation back. After nearly two hours of being spoken at, not to, I rose abruptly.

"I really must go. Nice to meet you both. I hope your trip continues along well."

Then I fled.

I hadn't been back in my cabin long when there was a soft knock on the door. I peered around and found Anne there.

"Hi Anne."

"Oh, Janine. Sorry to intrude. Jack said you should have taken your light beer. He appreciated the heavy ones you brought, but doesn't drink this. I thought I'd return them to you."

I opened the door. "Come on in," I said.

Anne was one of those women who had an abundance of grace. She moved elegantly with a straight spine. She was softly spoken, her words coming slowly and thoughtfully. There was nothing brash or loud about her, and there was also no nonsense. I liked her a lot.

"Take a seat. Jack said you'd like some female company, but then we didn't get a chance to talk."

She compressed her lips. "Janine, I never, ever get the chance to talk. Words start spilling out of that man first thing in the morning and they don't stop until he goes to sleep. There should be a limit on how many words can be said by one person in one day!"

I smiled. "How long have you two been married?"

"Married. Heaven forbid! No, he's just my next door neighbour. He lost his wife recently and, well, my Mark passed away two and a half years ago."

"Oh, I see."

"Jack and his wife had planned this trip for years. He still wanted to go but needed someone to go with him. I know why, now. He needs someone to talk to!"

I laughed. "Oh, dear!"

"Oh dear, indeed. He's driving me mad. It's awful in the caravan because, although we have separate berths, he can still talk to me all the time. At least in the cabin here there is a separate room."

"Yes, he said you were fed up with the caravan."

Something about Anne made me want to talk to her, which was rare for me. We started discussing generalities and then my reasons for making the trip. I skirted around the real reason, telling her instead about the book I was writing. She was fascinated and asked many questions.

We heard a noise at the door and realised Jack had come over. "Anne, are you coming to dinner?"

Anne looked at me and whispered, "Is it okay if I stay here a while longer?"

"As long as you like. I'm enjoying your company."

She went to the door and said she would have dinner with me. Jack didn't sound too pleased, but went away. "He'll find someone to talk to in the bar," she said with satisfaction.

We settled back down in our seats and I wondered about dinner. I wasn't hungry, and Anne said she wasn't either.

"I don't eat a lot and we had some snacks with drinks earlier. Now, tell me all about your writing."

Hours later there was another knock at the door.

"Just me! Anne, I'm going to bed. Are you coming?"

She smiled at me and winked.

"We're just in a deep conversation about something. Go to bed and I'll be in soon."

"Okay, but don't forget our early start in the morning."

We heard him clump his way down the metal stairs.

I realised I had been talking about my writing non-stop for a long time. Anne had been clever in drawing conversation from me.

"Anne, I'm sorry. I've been talking your ears off. I'm as bad as Jack."

"No, I was very interested. I haven't told you about what I do for a living?"

I shook my head.

"And Jack didn't either?"

"No?"

"I'm actually an editor for a major publishing house. I was really interested in what you were telling me about your novels."

I could feel my face grow hot.

"Oh, now I've embarrassed you. Let me tell you some things. There are a lot of people like you who write for the sheer joy of writing. They do it for pleasure and not for profit. In my experience, people like you often have a rare and wonderful talent. I would like to read your work."

"Oh, no! Most of my novels are still rough drafts."

"I'd bet anything they are still in very good shape. You have a particular way of talking which makes me believe that your writing wouldn't be weighed down by too much description. You'd be more like Hemingway than Proust. Is that true?"

"Yes, I guess that's true."

"If I give you my email address, will you send them to me, please?"

I blew out my cheeks and sat back in the seat. "I guess I could do that."

"And while I'm asking for favours, there's one more."

"Yes?"

"I want to write my story for you. For your latest work. If you give me some paper, I'll sit here and write it now."

It was my own curiosity that made me agree. I wanted to learn more about this intelligent and gracious woman. I fetched a notebook and a good pen.

# ANNE'S STORY

I have often thought that my story should be told, that I should put pen to paper and ensure that what happened in my life will not die with me, that the readers of this tale will become witnesses to an extraordinary love story.

Mark and I had no children, you see. We tried for a few years but then gave up with only mild regret. So there is no-one, therefore, who can pass on our story, give testament to such an amazing union.

This is a quiet and simple story. He and I met at a book signing. I wasn't his editor, but was representing the company for that event. I introduced myself and shook his hand, feeling a strange current of energy pass between us. I was surprised by this and thought I also saw surprise on his face.

After he had signed all the books for those people standing in the long queue and talked to the stragglers, I invited him for a drink. He was from Melbourne, and it was quite in order for me to entertain him on behalf of the company. We went to a bar in the Opera House precinct that had views of Circular Quay and the Harbour Bridge. We sat and admired the view, commenting on the ferries, busily going this way and that.

We began trading life stories and found ourselves talking freely about very private matters. I was still single, my career not allowing me much time for socialising or settling down. I had been 'seeing' someone for a while, but it was mainly for convenience.

Mark was married with grown-up children. They had all left home, the last one just recently, and in that newly empty house, he and his wife were forced into an intimacy that neither enjoyed. There was no romance, passion, or even affection left on either side. He had come to the conclusion, however, that this was his lot. He would slide into old age and eventual death without experiencing any more excitement or passion.

The sudden and totally unexpected acceptance of his novel had propelled him onto a different course. This was his only work to date, fiction, but strongly autobiographical as many good novels are. It was a coming of age story, funny, sad and thrilling. We rescued it from the slush pile, he did some minor re-writes, and soon it went to print. It won a small literary award and then he became mildly famous. He found this experience both exhilarating and bewildering.

At some point during his story he touched me on the hand to emphasise a point. I felt that surge again. This time we acknowledged it to each other in wonder.

We quickly fell deeply and profoundly in love. Such a love cannot be contained, as much as we tried. It was in this way that I became the 'other woman', a role I never intended to play. We saw each other as often as we could, made possible by his tour of the capital cities and my role in the publishing firm. I had absolutely no expectation that he would leave his wife, while he suffered all manner of emotions about seeing me behind her back.

I was the first to decide we shouldn't see each other any more. The suddenness and severity of my feelings for him were troubling me and I knew we were headed for stormy waters. When I was with him my doubts disappeared, but as soon as he was gone, they returned in full force. These highs and lows were debilitating. I felt they were harming my well-being and told him so one day over the telephone. I told him we were over.

He sounded distressed, but was understanding. By the

end of the call he was almost philosophical, agreeing that it was probably the best thing. Later that day he rang back to say that he, in fact, could not come to terms with that decision and to ask me to please reconsider. I had spent a miserable day, wondering how I'd cope with the loss of such a great love. I burst into tears and agreed to meet him to discuss it further. Our affair continued.

He was the next to call it off. There had been a problem in his family, a private matter that I won't write about. It made him feel guilty, and he phoned to say he couldn't see me anymore. I told him, gently, that I understood and hung up. I listened to sad break-up songs for the rest of the day. At six in the afternoon I got another call from him to say he found he couldn't manage without me in his life and he was sorry. Could he come and see me so we could talk about it further?

I remember hearing his car pull up and watching through a gauzy curtain as he got out and stretched his sore back. He walked quickly to my door, and I met him there. He opened his arms, and I slid gratefully into their warmth. This was where I belonged.

Two months later it was my turn again. I could feel the rebellion rising in me, the hatred of the secrecy and dishonesty. I found that, even though I cherished my independence, I now hated him leaving me to return to his other life. Recognising that this was a dangerous and unhealthy state of mind, I again told him we wouldn't be seeing each other again. Once again he agreed and we said goodbye.

I didn't ask him to leave his wife. Not once. I didn't even hint at it. Occasionally he would talk about a life where we would be together, but I took that as fantasising out loud. So when he rang to tell me that he had decided to do just that, so we could be together, it took my breath away.

Let me tell you something: it was the bravest act I've witnessed in my life.

All hell broke loose. His children reacted badly; lifetime friends turned their backs on him. His wife was on the verge of a breakdown. He wobbled for a time, caught between his old life and the new one with me, but in the end he became resolute and thumbed his nose at those people who decided to take the moral high ground.

I suffered some condemnation as well, mostly at my workplace. I was a senior editor in the company that published his novel. There was talk of conflict, of a need to find another place for me within the organisation. Eventually it all calmed down, however, and I stayed where

I was.

Eight blissful years passed. I can't begin to tell you how happy we were. It didn't matter that friends had deserted us - we really just didn't need them or anybody else. At the end of every day we would sink into each other's arms, and the world would go away and leave us in peace. I didn't know that such a relationship could exist.

I loved our evenings the most. After dinner we would take up our customary positions at each end of the long sofa, facing one another. Our legs would intertwine as we read or wrote or did whatever we felt like. We would be mostly silent, only saying things softly as they came to mind: it might be me commenting on an especially well written manuscript I was reading, or Mark telling me of a thought or idea he just had.

Television was anathema to both of us, and the screen remained blank. The only sound was soft classical music coming from the speakers of the sound system.

Sunday mornings were wonderful, too. We would sleep in until late and still take a long time to rise from the bed. We would eat breakfast on our deck, which by that time would have the sun shining on it, while reading the weekend papers.

Pancreatic cancer was the thief that came in the night

and stole Mark from me. It was a protracted and terrible illness that you wouldn't wish on your worst enemy. At least there wasn't much pain, not until the last stages. This brave and loving man was taken from me nearly ten years after he gave up everything to be with me. Some would say he got his just deserts. I know that the Gods aren't that malicious.

The subject of grief has been well documented throughout the span of man's existence and I have read a great deal of it, but as I sat by Mark's hospital bed, his newly lifeless hand in mine, I realised that no words exist to describe what I felt at that moment: the knowledge that from that time forward my life would be reduced to a tragic black and white facsimile of the original, that a dark cloud had drifted across the sun and would linger there for eternity. I knew I would never recover from this loss.

In some cultures it is considered normal for those grieving to tear their hair and clothing, and scream. Others simply throw themselves on the funeral pyre of those they love, but that's not the Anglo-Saxon way. I maintained a 'stiff upper lip' and carried on projecting an illusion of bravery, only giving in to grief while sheltered by the privacy of my own company.

There have been men since who have shown an interest in filling the gap caused by Mark's absence, but as none were Mark I dismissed them without a second glance.

The moral of my story is simple: love arrives without regard for time and place. It just comes. Sometimes it will cause upset and distress to others, but if it is a true love it cannot be denied. It just is.

Anne

# CHAPTER THIRTEEN

I woke with a sore neck and stiff back. I hadn't made it into bed, but had fallen asleep on the sofa while Anne wrote. Raising myself on one elbow, I looked around and saw some pages lying on the small dining table. I also discovered that Anne had covered me with a blanket and put a pillow under my head.

I was impatient to see her story. Glancing over it I admired her style which was matter of fact, but still able to evoke emotion. It was gentle, without any great upsets or epiphanies. She had loved well and had been loved well. It was a worthy story for inclusion.

Beside her story was a single sheet which read, in large capital letters, "SEND ME YOUR STORIES!" Her email address and mobile phone number were written underneath. I smiled.

The best image I had of her was taken while she was

writing. She had looked up and smiled at me through the camera lens, her head tilted. The photograph projected her natural warmth.

My watch said nine-fifteen. I'd slept in. I looked out the door and saw that Jack and Anne's cabin was deserted, the car and caravan gone. An early start indeed.

I had an easy day in front of me: a three and a half hour drive to Katherine. I packed quickly, checked out, and picked up my spare tyre.

As I drove away from the service station I saw a sight that caused a knot in my stomach. It was a young man, walking with his arm outstretched and thumb extended. He looked just like my son, Michael. It was all in the posture and colouring, his dark hair, olive skin, and easy grace. I looked at him closely, and he looked back at me. I saw then that he was a few years older than my son, but there was a very strong resemblance. I drove away, shaking.

What can I tell you about my son? The fact is I can't tell you a great deal. We were very close in his early years, but as time went by and he found his independence, he and I broke that gossamer thread of emotional engagement that we had shared. Or should I say, he broke it. I think he took after his father. One day he realised that he just didn't *need* me in the same way and when he looked at me, it was without focus.

Was I distraught? Absolutely not. You must remember that motherhood hadn't come naturally to me. When he made me feel less like a mother, I felt lighter. I wasn't the sort of woman who chased after her son, trying to pick up some discarded crumbs of attention or affection. When I looked at him it was also in an unfocused way.

By the time I left David, it was with an emotional freedom from both of them. When he told me that I couldn't take Michael, I was puzzled. I had never intended to. David had said it to try to hurt me, but to me he was just stating the obvious. No, I couldn't take him. It never occurred to me to do so.

Michael was big like his father, but better looking. He played Rugby Union and had a large circle of friends, both male and female. He ignored his father's plea to join his company as an apprentice electrician and instead focused on getting the right OP score so he could enter university to study law.

When people disappear from my radar, they really disappear. When I left David, I basically forgot that both he and Michael even existed. I know some people will find this disturbing, but it is the plain truth. It was with a shock, therefore, that after six months or so I found David on the other end of a call, wanting to talk about Michael.

"What sort of mother are you? You haven't even rung him since you left!"

"You told me not to."

"I didn't expect you to take it literally. You're his mother, for Christ's sake!"

"Has Michael complained?"

"No, but that's not the point. I think he should be spending some time with you."

"Oh?"

"Perhaps every second weekend or something."

"What does Michael think of this?"

"I haven't discussed it with him."

"Talk to him and ring me back after you have." I hung up in his ear.

Chris laughed. "He's got a new love interest!"

"Eh?"

"David. I reckon this has come about because he has a new girlfriend. They want some time alone."

I shook my head with wonder. How did she know this stuff?

David rang back later that evening.

"Yeah, he's going to spend every second weekend with you."

"Do you have a new girlfriend?"

There was silence at the other end.

"I see. You want private time with her, and that's what this is all about. Right?"

"Yeah, well," he coughed. "There is this woman—"

I interrupted. "Anyway, if he wants to come he is welcome. He's old enough to make the arrangements with me directly. He can phone, text or email. We're busy this weekend but it can start the one after. I'll get a room ready for him."

The thing is that he loved it at our place. He asked for a key and from time to time I'd come home and find him there, unexpectedly. Sometimes I'd find him and Chris playing cards or video games. My only rule was that he let his father know where he was.

One day I had a phone call from David. His new girlfriend, Jodie, was going to move in with him. Jodie thought I might want to meet the woman who would be partly responsible for raising her son. They invited me around for a drink. I suggested that Chris come along as well. Perhaps suggested is the wrong word; I demanded the invitation include her. On an unusually chilly Sunday, we arrived at David's house, armed with drinks and nibbles.

Jodie was perfect for David. She was warm and friendly and funny. She had long blonde hair which was straightened as was demanded by the latest fashion trend. She was as brown as a berry, and I guessed she spent a lot of time in tanning salons.

Michael had a girl there. Kelly was sweet and beautiful, and looked at Michael in adoration. They touched each other often in the way of new lovers, and it took me some time to realise, with awe, that he was now a sexual being.

Late in the afternoon I excused myself to go to the bathroom. When I came out, Michael was standing waiting for me. "Mum, I wanted to ask you something."

"What is it?"

"Can I live with you now, full time? Dad and Jodie make me sick."

"What does your father say?"

"I haven't asked him yet. I hoped you might."

"If your father agrees, then yes, you can move over to our place. But you have to ask him."

Apparently it wasn't a problem, and Michael moved in with us for his university years.

I sighed as I lowered myself into the clear, warm waters of Bitter Springs. I'd gone to the Mataranka Thermal Pool first, but found it crowded, mostly with older couples. Bitter Springs was deeper and more natural looking, with the added benefit of an adjoining stream, which I followed for quite a distance before finding a ladder to climb out. From there I had looped back and returned to the main pool with pleasure. I was told that the temperature of the springs was 34 degrees Celsius and it felt divine. It was hard to leave; I could have stayed there all day.

Mataranka was the setting of *We of the Never Never,* and I detoured to Elsey Cemetery to visit the memorial to the author. Her husband's grave was there as well. Jeannie Gunn had loved this region and wrote so eloquently about her experiences living there, her words infused with fondness.

Soon I was on the road to Katherine. I noticed that I wasn't sitting well in my own skin. Since thinking about menopause the previous day, heaviness had settled on my spirit, and I wasn't able to shake it. While talking to Anne it had receded, but was now back in full force. There was blackness, just out of range of my vision, sitting there menacingly. I felt its suffocating presence.

I reached Katherine after one and a half hours. This time I had pre-booked my accommodation and had selected a superior room. My shoulders were tense and my legs heavy. I put my bags down and lay on the bed and stared at the ceiling. Interaction with other people was not an option. Instead I read until I was hungry and then ordered room service. I read some more and turned out the light, hoping the next day would be better.

As I drove out of Katherine the next morning, I was shocked to see the young man that looked like Michael. He was standing in the same pose as when I saw him at Daly Waters. I thought of giving him a ride, but dismissed it as foolhardy. By the time I had travelled another kilometre, I had changed my mind. If I could charge men for my sexual favours, I could pick up hitch-hikers.

I turned and went back. Then I turned again and pulled up beside him. "Where are you going?"

"Darwin."

I was surprised by his Irish accent. He looked so much like my son that I expected him to sound the same.

"Hop in."

He threw his backpack in the rear and took the front

passenger seat. "I'm most grateful, Miss," he said with his delightful lilt. "The name's Dairmund."

Having him there helped my mood. He talked constantly, but I didn't find it irritating. He was in Australia on a working holiday visa and was hoping to find a job as a barman in Darwin.

The road was good, and, although there was still red soil, there were trees lining the road, so the effect was less desolate. The four hours passed quickly, and soon we were on the outskirts of the city. Dairmund indicated where I could drop him off. The car seemed very empty without him.

I had decided to stay several days in Darwin, so selected one of their top hotels and took a deluxe room. Within minutes of checking in I was taking advantage of their high-speed internet to catch up on some necessary tasks. I began with my finances. I had hardly touched the money in my accounts. My pay and holiday loading had landed into the savings account. My expenses had been low. I could splurge a bit in Darwin.

I went to Google Maps and checked out the drive from Darwin to Broome. I realised I didn't want to do it. I sat back in my seat and considered my options. There were several, but I settled on the easiest. I would send the car back to Brisbane by truck and fly to Broome in a few days. As soon as I made the decision I felt better.

My mobile made a sound. I looked and saw it was a text from an unknown person. "RU in Darwin, yet? Tom."

Tom. I tried to recall the features of the road train driver, without much success. What I did remember was how at ease I had felt with him.

I sent a reply, telling him the name of the hotel.

"Just driving in. C U in lobby at 7?"

"OK."

I emptied out my bag and looked at my clothes selection. This was the capital city of the Northern Territory and I was staying in one of the top hotels. A red-tinged t-shirt and jeans just wouldn't make the grade. I bit my lip, then grabbed my purse and ran out the door.


"Just a light beer, thanks."

The barman reached under the counter and produced a stubby. He poured the beer into a frosted glass with a flourish and slid it across the counter to me. I had arrived early, wanting a drink to calm my nerves. I sat at a table which could be seen easily from the lobby.

I found the quiet murmur of voices from other

patrons soothing. Looking around the room I saw several business men in groups of two, their ties loosened. If I felt like picking someone up later, this would be a good bar in which to do it.

I looked at the men with interest. Most were around my own age, some with soft stomachs that hung over their belts. Suddenly I found them repulsive.

"Hello, there!"

I swung around to find Tom in front of me. I had been so engrossed in the other men that I hadn't seen him approaching.

"Hi Tom. I've just got a drink. I'll get you one as well."

His face turned red. "Nah. I don't let girls buy me drinks. I'll get my own."

I smiled. Chivalry wasn't dead in the bush.

He returned with a beer for each of us and some nuts.

"What do ya wanna do t'night?"

"Oh, I don't know. Just a quiet meal would do me fine."

"Do ya like seafood, then?"

"Definitely."

He nodded sagely and took a big gulp of beer.

We spoke about our respective travels since we'd first met. I related the story of the flat tyre which didn't elicit much of a response from him.

"I get 'em all the time in the truck."

"Oh, I suppose so."

He told me about where he lived and a story about his neighbours. It was long-winded and I began to feel restless. I wondered about finding a topic of interest to both of us, then realised with a sinking feeling that there probably wasn't one. If I had better social skills I could have overcome this.

A silence fell over us. I decided I couldn't get through a whole dinner with this man.

"Hey, I'm not feeling very well tonight. Do you mind if we give dinner a miss?"

His eyes widened and the corners of his mouth turned down.

"That's no good. I had high hopes for our night out."

"Sorry Tom. I'm not used to driving long distances like you. I think I've been overdoing it."

I made a sign to the barman and he brought me the bill for my beer.

I said goodbye to Tom and left the bar quickly.

I wrote this from John Four's room that night:

I'm sitting in the near-darkness trying to write this. John Four didn't want the lights on while we had sex and I'm not sure why. Did he have a disfigurement or some bad tattoos? Some light is spilling from the bathroom, but it is still quite dark.

I charged him two hundred dollars for the hour. He had to go to a teller machine and get it, and it took him so long I thought he'd bolted. While I waited, I sat at the bar and looked at myself in the mirror behind the bottles. The soft lights in the lobby bar were flattering, and, with the dress I'd purchased hurriedly for my date with Tom, I thought I looked nice.

When we came to John Four's room, he spent some time putting his things away, and then he went to the bathroom for around five minutes. I reached into my bag for a condom and some lubricant and then sat, swinging my legs until he came out again. He stood before me, touching my hair. He asked me to undress and get into bed. Once I'd finished that, he turned out the lights, undressed and slid in beside me.

He wanted to talk first, to get to know me a little. I told him that talking isn't something I do.

He was flaccid. I played with him gently, holding him close as I did so. Gradually he became more erect. His penis was very small and the condom wasn't tight on him. He entered me and came within an instant, almost sobbing as he did so. Then he fell asleep on top of me.

He wasn't a large man so this wasn't hurting me, but I felt like

*I was suffocating. I rolled him off me and he slumped like a sack of potatoes. I lay there for a few minutes and then went to the bathroom, closing the door before turning on the light so I wouldn't disturb him. I washed and put on the hotel bathrobe.*

*There is still forty minutes left of the hour. I'll use this time to compile a list of things to do tomorrow.*

I wrote this from my room later that night:

*I was left unsatisfied after my encounter with John Four. I'm not talking about sexually, although I certainly didn't gain any satisfaction from him. Since leaving Brisbane I have had an overwhelming desire to experience sex in all its forms. Is it because of what I witnessed there? Since leaving home I've more than doubled the number of men I've been with. Am I trying to prove something to myself? Am I trying to overcome what I suspect is naivety?*

*After leaving John Four's room I went back down to the bar and looked around with disappointment. Not much action there. I left the hotel and walked up the street until I found a bar with bouncers standing out the front. I knew I would hate the noise inside, but I didn't plan on staying long.*

*I picked someone different from the rest, and precisely for that reason. His hair was tied back in a ponytail and he had a small beard. He seemed edgy, which matched my mood. He appeared to be alone, so I stood near him and sipped a drink. He looked at his mobile phone a few times, and then saw me. Soon we were talking. He didn't have a room and I wasn't about to take him back to mine. We went to his car. He drove to a secluded place and he started trying to pleasure me, but I stopped him. We hadn't spoken about money and I didn't raise that subject at all. I just unbuttoned his jeans and straddled him - no condom. I guided his hand to where he should rub me while I rode him, and then when I felt the orgasm rising I asked him to put his hands around my throat. He came right then and spoiled the moment. He started trying to rub me again and said he could get me to that place again and do what I wanted, but I just felt sad and wanted to go back to my room.*

*He drove me back silently and neither of us said goodbye as I left the car.*

*Erotic asphyxiation is what I had tried to get him to do. I had researched it. I thought it sounded like a weird way to get pleasure.*

# CHAPTER FOURTEEN

The man who came to fix the windscreen of the car was surly. I don't know what his problem was, but I found it unnerving to have to deal with him. I ended up paying him upfront, and told him to return the keys to reception so I didn't have to wait for the job to be done.

The concierge was helpful in getting the car cleaned and detailed. I just left the keys with him, and several hours later there was a knock on the door. He had brought the keys back personally.

Finding a car-carrier to Brisbane was harder to accomplish, especially since I wanted to get the SUV there quickly. I ended up settling on one of the major companies and told them I'd pre-pay. I inspected the car, noting happily that the detailers had done a wonderful job of removing all the red dust from the interior. The outside didn't concern me because it would get dirty again on the truck. I double-checked that I'd taken all my gear out, and then left a note on the dashboard that said, "Thanks, Boss."

I wondered what the Boss would think when the SUV arrived back in Brisbane. I'd promised to stay in touch, but couldn't quite bring myself to call him.

I was so lucky to have landed a job in his company. When he first introduced himself to me at the interview, he held out his hand and said, "Hi, I'm the Boss." Somehow that appealed to my sense of humour, and from that time on I'd referred to him by that title.

Plain-speaking people, without hidden agendas or tendency to play psychological games, will always win a place in my heart. The Boss was that sort of man. He said what he thought, he did what he said he was going to, and he was always balanced in his decision making. I felt safe with him, despite his loud, brash exterior.

I had only been working there for a week or so before I began sussing out the IT Department. The IT Manager, Derek, was someone I instinctively understood. He was very quiet, almost to the point of being introverted. If, however, you got onto his wavelength by having knowledge of IT, he opened up like a tulip in springtime.

I spent a lot of my lunch hours in the IT department, learning about the company's methods of networking and also about the all-important DMS, or Dealer Management System. Derek, once he learned I was up for it, happily taught me as much as I wanted to learn. Soon I was spending my spare time helping him. After I'd been working at the dealership for a few months, I'd slip into the IT Department whenever my own duties were slow, or when the Boss was away.

It had to get back to the Boss, of course. I was called into his office and asked what it was all about. The way he posed his questions made me wonder if he thought Derek and I had formed a 'special friendship'. I was quick to point out my background in IT and told him that having another person knowledgeable about the computer system could only be good for his business. He didn't seem convinced, so I had cut down on my IT activities.

One day I saw Derek and the Boss go into the boardroom for a meeting. I heard the Boss raise his voice, and soon after Derek left with his head lowered. The Boss called me in.

"Derek wants you transferred to his department as his 2IC."

"Really?" I said. I felt a huge smile forming on my face.

It didn't last long.

"I told him that you are the smartest person in Admin and that I needed to keep you close because you make me look smarter."

I looked at him for some time, then down at my shoes.

"Aw, don't be upset. How about we schedule a few hours a week when you can help him?"

"Can I?"

"Yeah, I think I was too rough on the poor guy. I think he nearly shat himself."

We both smiled.

"I could go there on Tuesday mornings and Friday afternoons when you play golf. How's that?"

"Yeah, I suppose so. As long as your usual work doesn't suffer."

"No way."

"Yeah, I know. You're a good gal. I reckon you'd stay behind every night for a few hours to do your own work if it meant being let loose in IT."

He was right.

So the new plan was put in place, and I spent as much time as I dared with Derek, helping him maintain the computer system. I implemented a weekly maintenance program, like I had in my previous job, and would often slip in on a Saturday morning to do more work on the system. Derek was very happy indeed.

Sometimes he would ring me. "Hey, I've got a problem. Can you come over when you've got a minute?" I'd wait until the Boss went away from his desk, whether it was for a meeting or another purpose, and I'd sneak over to IT and help out. A couple of times Derek received an angry call and would have to send me back.

Once, at a function I had organised and so had to attend, the Boss had a lot to drink and became a bit too friendly. I rebuffed him gently and he shrugged and walked away. That was the only time anything like this happened and neither of us referred to it again.

The thing about the Boss and I is that we have a high mutual regard for each other. I feel warmth from him and it is reciprocated. It's rare that I connect myself so wholeheartedly to a person, but I did with the Boss. We were loyal to each other, in a working sense. When David was trying to force me to resign, I resisted very stubbornly.

In the time I'd worked for him, I had gone from a single woman, recently moved to Brisbane, to a wife and mother. I had seen my son grow, and then grow away from me. Then my husband and I grew apart. My job was what I felt anchored me; it was the part of my life that remained constant.

The problem now was Chris. I'd made that age-old mistake. An old motor-industry saying summed it up. "Don't get your meat where you get your bread and butter." Wiser words have never been spoken.

For the rest of that day I stayed in the room, enjoying the fast internet access. I had sent all my clothes, except the new dress, to the laundry, and just lolled around in the bathrobe the hotel provided. I booked a flight to Broome for two days later, which would get me there well in time for the full moon.

The darkness I'd felt for a few days was always at my elbow, regardless of what I was doing. It felt like a person, or an animal. Originally it was menacing, but it had changed character and now felt more seductive. A song came to mind, mournful and gut-wrenching. I went to a music site and downloaded it, and while it played I searched for the lyrics.

I played the song over and over again. I admired the singer's voice while drowning in her misery. I went and lay on the bed, turned on my side, and brought my knees up to my chest. The lyrics resonated within me.

Until then I had handled my grief. I had stayed busy and pushed the bad thoughts away. That afternoon, lying on the bed, wrapped in the bathrobe, I gave in to the sadness and negativity. I brought Chris to the uppermost part of my mind. I examined her as if she were there with me, I could see her hair, eyes and body. I could almost smell her. I could hear her calming voice, soothing me when I was distressed. I could hear her laugh, which sometimes bordered on maniacal. I saw her watching a goofy, brainless Hollywood movie while spilling popcorn and hooting with delight. I saw her at work with the ring of admirers who stood close in order to bask in her radiant light.

I groaned and rolled over. "Oh, Chris...Chris...what have you done to us?" I kept saying this over and over as I tossed from side to side.

# CHAPTER FIFTEEN

There was no aerobridge for boarding the flight to Broome. It was done the old-fashioned way, with passengers having to cross the tarmac to the aircraft and then climb the stairs to the cabin.

I winced as I took each step, feeling the injuries that I had received during the previous night's activities. This time I had charged Johns Six and Seven one thousand dollars for two hours. They both took me at the same time and I hadn't demanded any restrictions.

I didn't take a lot of notice of the men. I remember one being coltish with an overlarge penis, which caused me tissue damage. The other was slender and smelled nice. They poked and prodded incessantly, entering and withdrawing frequently. I left as soon as the two hours were up. When I got back to my room, I pushed the $1,000 into the flap of my backpack, where it joined the last two lots of earnings. I looked at the money with revulsion and quickly zipped the flap closed.

I couldn't write anything afterwards; the words just wouldn't come.

As I watched the parched earth pass below me, I was grateful I had decided to send the SUV back to Brisbane. Driving under such conditions was an experience, but I was no longer in the mood for challenges. I was feeling the weight of my humanity. The darkness was closer now; I could feel its breath on my neck.

The Kunanurra stop-over was brief, and we soon resumed the flight towards Broome. I was sitting in the third row with a vacant seat beside me, for which I was grateful. I didn't want to talk to anyone. I wasn't even interested in their stories. Why would I be when I couldn't even work out my own?

The day before, from waking in the Darwin hotel room to the time I went down to the bar in the evening, was somehow missing. I knew I hadn't left the room all day and mostly just lay on the bed, staring at the ceiling. I had written some pages early in the day and, while on this flight, decided to re-read them.

"*Four people told me their stories and I don't know why. Was this a message from the Universe? Was it a reminder that I am a valid member of the human race? If that was the intent, then it was a failure.*

*I listened to these stories and recognised their value. I recorded them for others to read, knowing they held important messages. What these stories and these people didn't do was touch me. I didn't feel for them. I didn't want to talk further to the story tellers, to befriend them or tell them anything of my own life. I heard. I recorded. I commented. I photographed. I left. That is all.*

*I lie here and imagine myself as a single-celled organism, floating in the ocean at the dawn of time. There are millions of cells the same as me and they are attracted to each other, colliding and clumping together to form colonies.*

*I don't attract other cells. When they float toward me, or accidentally bump into me, they are repelled. I have a slippery outer membrane that can't be adhered to. I have a field about me that repels the others as though we were magnets with the same polarity. The others cluster and colonise and I am left alone.*

*I see myself as a recently formed star. Something went wrong during my creation, and I never shone brilliantly. My solar system didn't flourish. I see Christine as another star. At the moment of her creation she burst forth, brilliant and almost shocking in her magnificence. For a time I was close enough to feel her warmth; share her fire. It made my own pitiful light glow brighter momentarily. Now that she is gone my fire is all but extinguished. I believe I will eventually become a dead star, imploding and morphing into a black hole. In this form I will suck all the worthless debris from the universe into my centre, into my soul."*

The aircraft began its descent. I closed the notebook and ran my fingers over the cover while looking out the window, sightlessly.

I was dropping toward the earth in order to visit the moon.

As I stumbled through the door to my apartment my bags fell to the floor. I walked the few steps to a sofa and sat down heavily, feeling a spear of pain through the lower part of my torso. Realising I was very thirsty, I pushed down with my arms to give my body leverage. In this way I rose from the sofa and walked to the kitchen.

I drank a full glass of water, and then walked around the room, noting the balcony with the view of Roebuck Bay. That's why I had selected this location and this particular suite; the website suggested I could view the Staircase to the Moon without leaving the apartment. It was expensive, being a two bedroom-two bathroom suite, but it was worth it.

I had reserved it for sixteen nights which take me to the no-moon night. I still couldn't see past that time.

After collecting my bags that were in a pile on the floor, I went through to the bedroom and threw them on the Queen bed. Every movement felt like it required a huge effort. I stowed everything, and then I lay down on my side and tucked my legs under my chest.

Even when I closed my eyes I could see the darkness at the edge of my vision. I could feel its long tentacles brushing my skin. As I lay then, on that first day in Broome, I could sense it moving, then felt it lying full-length behind me, trying to spoon into my back. I repelled it with what little energy I had left, and it contracted and moved back to its customary place, near my elbow.

This is what I wrote in my notebook the next morning:

*My room overlooks a resort-style pool. A mother is gently coaxing her toddler to swim, while a baby in a pram, sitting in the shade of one of the resort umbrellas, watches with bemused disinterest. A man enters the enclosure and dives in the deep end, swimming underwater until he bobs up under the mother and child. The mother seems to admonish him gently and he begins lazy laps of the pool, cutting expertly through the warm tropical water.*

*I know I am blessed to be here, but peace is now a fictional state. It eludes me artfully, dodging this way and that when I try to catch it.*

*I crave peace; that is all I want. I have driven right across Australia to find it, and have to some small extent. It is not enough.*

*What am I actually seeking? It seems to be some sort of closure or resolution. To what? I don't know. I just know that the no moon night will be a catalyst. In what way? I don't know. All I can say is this - I cannot see beyond that no-moon night. My journey will be over. I need to have found peace by then.*

"Hello.....er.....hello!" Someone was calling from behind me, and I could hear their feet running. Looking around I was surprised to see the troubled woman from Barcaldine trying to catch up to me.

"I saw ya in the distance and I wanted to come and say 'ello."

I didn't know what to say for a minute. I just looked at her.

"You do remember me, don't ya? I'm Nikki."

"Yes, sorry. Don't mind me. You're a long way from Barcaldine."

"Yeah, well ya know how ya found out that Western Australia was okay for, " she looked around and lowered her voice, "terminations. I decided to come 'ere and have one."

"Oh, okay. When?"

"Tomorrow afternoon. I've already been to see 'em and have set it all up."

"It's a big coincidence, meeting you again."

"No, I remembered you saying you were driving here. At least I had a chance of running into someone I knew."

I nodded.

"I sort of used you as like an alibi, see. Said I needed a break and was going to meet a friend. Said I'd met you in the pub."

"And that worked?"

"Not really, but I'm 'ere."

I motioned her into a cafe and we ordered coffee.

"Yeah," she said, "I didn't even know if ya would be here yet. It's a small town, so I figured if ya were, I'd bump into ya somewhere."

I didn't quite know what to think about this latest development. I had planned just to stay alone and had only emerged from my room for some necessities. My lack of enthusiasm must have shown.

"Gee. I'm sorry," she said. "Ya must be wonderin' what I expect of you. I just wanted to see a friendly face, that's all. Don't think I want ya to hold my hand or anything'."

I roused myself a bit. "Sorry, I'm just not myself at the moment. Where are you staying?"

"Just in a cabin at the caravan park."

"Oh, okay. What's it like?"

She looked away. "Oh, it's okay."

"Tell me the truth."

Her eyes stayed averted. "No, really. It's okay. It's only for a few nights."

The reason I always stay in good hotels is mainly because of the sensory problems I have. Bad smells, bad lighting, even patterned wallpaper can make me feel ill. I have a horror of cheap sheets that feel unclean, or of carpet that is stained. Good hotels have lighting you can control, crisp cotton sheets, and they always smell nice. They also usually have good staff who can help with any problems I might have.

She changed the subject, telling me all about her journey to Broome and the nice doctor who would undertake the procedure. She'd met with him the day before, and they had discussed what would happen. We talked about the Staircase to the Moon. It would be at its best just after her procedure, so she didn't think she would be able to see it.

"So what time are you having it done?"

She sighed. "The morning will be basically free. I have to fast, and then turn up there at two o'clock. They'll check me over again and then do the…the…you know. I'll be allowed to go after the anaesthetic wears off."

"Back to your room at the Caravan Park."

"Yeah, that's right."

My mind went back to the suite I was staying in with its two bedrooms. I knew that I should offer one room to her, but the words wouldn't leave my mouth.

"Hey, I'm going to be busy the next few days. I'm writing a book and have a deadline."

"Oh, yeah. I understand."

"By the time I'm finished you'll probably be gone."

"Yeah, I'll be heading back in a couple of days."

I had a thought. "But I'd like to help you in one way." I reached into my backpack and produced the wad of notes I'd collected from the last few men.

Nikki held up her hands in a blocking protest movement.

"No, Nikki. Let me tell you something. I came by this money in ways I'm not happy with. I never planned to keep it. Please take it and book yourself into somewhere really nice. Somewhere clean. It should be really, really clean. Okay?"

She chewed on her lip for a few minutes and then accepted the money.

Then I told her about the volume of stories, how I'd like to hear hers and, if it was suitable, include it in the book. I assured her that the names of people and places would be changed. No one would know it was her. She frowned and looked at me for a long time.

"Gee, I dunno....."

"Look, I don't even know if this book has the remotest chance of being published. If it is, I might want your story to be in it. I promise to protect you in every way."

She stared at the hands in her lap, her brow creased.

"Can I think about it? I'll let ya know."

"No problems. Where are you having the procedure done?"

"Just over there. That white building. See it? Upstairs."

"Okay. If I get enough work done tomorrow I might drop by in the afternoon. Okay?"

Her smile was radiant. "Gee...okay. Thanks!"

I had a list of things I needed immediately, then another list of items I'd eventually need during my stay. At the top of my immediate list were some chemist supplies. My session with the two men had upset the whole of my genital area. I felt very unwell and was worried about what infections I might be incubating.

The supermarket was surprisingly well stocked, and I wandered the aisles picking up items. I saw soy milk and wondered again about the state of my hormones. Should I start drinking it? I decided to look it up on the internet when I got back to the room. I thought cranberry juice could be medicinal.

It wasn't until I'd paid and left the supermarket that I realised I didn't have a car to load the groceries into. Catching a cab would be ludicrous - it wasn't that far. I re-adjusted my load and began walking.

I passed a bottle shop and looked in. There was only one person in there, and he was behind the counter. I stepped in and began looking at bottles. I'd heard about people drinking vodka with cranberry juice. I bought a small, flask-style bottle and added it to the load.

As soon as I got back to the room I opened the cranberry juice and poured a tall glass. I gulped down several mouthfuls, pulling a face as I did so. Next I reached for the vodka and added a splash. It didn't make much difference to the taste, but for some reason I felt good about having it.

Chris had queried me about my drinking not long after we started seeing each other.

"You don't drink much, do you?" It was a statement, not a question.

I shook my head.

"Why not? I drink like a fish!"

That was true. We laughed.

"I don't think alcohol is good for me."

"Ah, that's rubbish. The medical profession is always trotting that one out."

"No, I don't mean that."

"What do you mean?"

"Well, sometimes I say things that people take the wrong way. I don't mean them the way they sound, and whoever I say it to sort of looks at me a bit weird."

"I see. "

"And alcohol makes that worse. There have been a couple of times that I've really let myself go and have said some weird stuff. Since I've been with David, and we've had to socialise for business reasons, I've cut back to almost nothing."

"What sort of weird things do you say?"

"God...I can't even think of an example. I can't even tell you why it happens. I feel under pressure socially, and

I'm talking to someone, and I say something that's really from left field."

"Aunt Lily used to do that."

"Really?"

"Yeah, she'd shock everyone. I loved her for it."

In my apartment in Broome, by myself, I didn't have to worry about upsetting anyone. I could have a big drink.

I woke at some point with a dry mouth and a feeling like I was burning in my skin. I went to the bathroom and splashed water on my face and then drank a huge glass. This feeling was the other reason I didn't like drinking.

I had got through the whole flask, while sitting with my notebook, writing whatever came into my head. I was sure it would make interesting reading the next morning.

Sleep had deserted me. I lay in the gentle darkness, the near-full moon not in view, but lighting the sky nonetheless, and thought about the day. Meeting Nikki had helped me. Perhaps I should have asked her to stay to distract me from the horrors. Drinking the vodka had helped also, but its effects were only temporary. It all rushed back.

I got up and remade the bed, tucking the bottom sheet in tightly and re-aligning the top layers. When I climbed back in, I did so very carefully so everything would stay nice. I lay on my stomach and closed my eyes. Eventually I fell back to sleep.

# CHAPTER SIXTEEN

I pushed the glass door tentatively. I wasn't sure I was in the right place.

A receptionist looked up with a smile.

"Do you have a Nikki here? I'm a friend of hers."

"Oh, sure. She's just coming out of the anaesthetic now. Take a seat and I'll check if it's okay for you to go through."

Soon I was sitting beside Nikki, watching her struggle into consciousness.

"Hey....Janine. You came!"

"Yes. I couldn't have you enjoying all the fun."

Nikki smiled weakly. "I guess it's all over."

"I guess so."

"I suppose I should be really 'appy then."

"Maybe. Or maybe your hormones will play some

games for a couple of days."

"Yeah, I s'pose so."

"Did you get a better room?"

"Yeah, over at the big resort. Even got myself a fancier one. It's just amazing. Thanks heaps."

"That's what I like to hear."

She lapsed back into sleep for a while. I sat, thinking about Nikki having an abortion on a full moon, while I had a miscarriage on a no moon.

She stirred again. "You're still here! I'm so glad."

"You only went back to sleep for a little while. I'll stay and see you safely back to your room. Take your time."

I stepped onto the balcony of my apartment, juggling items in my arms. It was nearly time and I still had to get things ready.

I put the new bottle of vodka on the outdoor table, along with a fresh bottle of cranberry juice. I had cheese, nuts, crackers and fig paste. I went back inside and came out with the camera and tripod, notebook and fountain pen. I was all set.

Knowing enough about photography to realise that taking images of a rising full moon was tricky, I'd fiddled with the settings of the camera and saved two options as user-preferred settings. I placed the camera on the tripod, removed the lens cap and pointed the camera to where I thought the moon might rise. Then I poured myself a big drink.

My creativity had clicked back into gear that afternoon after Nikki told me her story, which had tumbled out after I'd helped her back to the hotel and into the oversized king bed. Her tale was so awful, yet almost poetic in its awfulness, like an old Italian opera.

I had almost run into my apartment to take notes and now, waiting for the moon to rise, I sat and reread them.

# NIKKI'S STORY

She was a true child of the outback; raised on a property where the nearest neighbour was more than an hour's drive away. She was an only child and a bit lonely. The closest neighbour had a son, Ben, who was around her age, and the two of them often spent time together or partnered each other to dances and other events.

Primary school was undertaken by remote means, but when it came time for secondary schooling, she was sent to a girls' boarding school in Victoria. Happiness was being home for the holidays, when she and Ben would ride off on adventures. She would grudgingly return to boarding school at the beginning of each term, dragging her heels and scowling. One year she realised that legally she didn't have to resume her schooling and flatly refused to do so.

Ben, however, continued his studies and went on to university. He made new friends, and she no longer got to see him regularly. One year he spent Christmas in London.

"Fancy that!" she told me with eyes wide. "To us at home it seemed like a miracle - going to London for Christmas!"

Nikki, in the meantime, was growing a bit wild. She would go to the dances and sneak drinks and cigarettes from the local boys. Often she would end the night having had sex with at least one of them. She was earning a reputation. "I was bored out of my brain at home. I couldn't just get a part-time job or anythin' 'cause we lived too far out, ya know?"

In Ben's third year of university he came home for the summer vacation. Nikki drove over to his parents' house in a frenzy of anticipation, only to find he'd brought a girl home with him. "I dunno why I thought he wouldn't have girlfriends. Silly, really."

The following July he came home alone. They spent time together and slipped back into their old friendship. He was different, though. "I guess he'd seen stuff I hadn't. Travel and things. He seemed like, I dunno, a movie star to me." On his last night before going back to university, they ended up having sex. "It was my idea and he just went along with it."

Ben gained his degree in veterinary science and worked 'on the coast' for two years. He'd still come home from time to time and would take Nikki out. They continued their sexual relationship, but it seemed like he treated it lightly.

His plan was always to become an outback vet and he finally had the opportunity to buy into a surgery in a town several hours' drive from her parent's property. They started seeing each other more and it seemed the next logical step was marriage. "We weren't madly in love or anythin'. It felt comfortable, like."

The first two years of marriage were busy. They had a small property a few kilometres out of town, and Nikki took on the duties of running the farm while Ben was at work. By the third year restlessness had begun to grow in her. Perhaps it was time to start a family.

One day her restlessness was worse than normal. She decided to spend a few hours in town. There was always plenty to do there, and she could talk to people. "I decided to get my hair cut in a new style. I'd been wearin' it the same way for years.'

It was while she was in the hairdresser's chair that she first saw him. "He went walking past the salon, looking in the window like he was tryin' to find someone. He looked at me and something happened inside me. It was the strangest feeling. We sorta looked at each other for a long time, then Deb, the hairdresser, said something to me and when I looked back he was gone. I wanted to get outta there quick, like. I told Deb I was in a 'urry and she finished as soon as she could."

Nikki ran out of the hairdresser's looking up and down the street, which was dusty and lit brightly by the midday sun. She remembered fumbling for her sunglasses and putting them on hurriedly, wanting to see if the stranger was still around. After a few minutes she walked slowly to the bank, trying to shrug off the disappointment. After completing her transactions she visited a café, chosen for its view of the street, for lunch. The stranger had disappeared.

Her last stop was the supermarket. She filled the trolley slowly, feeling like she was caught in a different time. "Once I went into shock after being thrown from my horse. I had the same feeling in that supermarket. It was weird."

Ice cream was on the list and she had to buy it last so it wouldn't melt on the drive home. She looked for her favourite brand and found there was only one container left, right at the back of the freezer. She reached for it, fumbling to grab an edge to bring it closer. A strong male arm reached over and retrieved it, handing it to her with a smile. It was the stranger. She watched as he walked past the checkouts, having purchased nothing.

The checkout operator, Suzi, was very chatty, but Nikki wasn't interested. She could see the man through the dirty windows, leaning against his car. While Suzi droned on about her boyfriend, Nikki noted the stranger's well-cut jeans and clean white shirt. He was older than she was, quite a bit older, but with his slicked back dark hair and tanned face, his slim waist and large chest, he was the most desirable man she had ever seen.

After walking out of the supermarket she said just two words to him:"Follow me." She started the Landcruiser with shaking hands. Her heart was beating wildly, and she could feel the sweat under her armpits. She pulled out into the street and watched in the rear vision mirror as he began following her.

"I couldn't think of anywhere to go, so I drove home. When we got there I just got out of the car and waited on the veranda for 'im to come to me. He walked up the steps and I moved towards 'im. I stood on my toes and kissed him and pressed my groin against his, you know? Then I felt something weird. I felt him hesitate for a second. I stopped and looked at him then kissed him again. I took his hand and led him into the house, into the lounge room. I undid his belt and pulled his jeans down, and took him in my mouth. Then he stopped me, turned me around and pushed in from behind. I was so wet; it was amazing. I'd never been like that before. He reached around and started to stroke me, you know, between the legs, while he moved in and out, and I just started to spasm, and my brain felt like it was going to explode. That was my first ever orgasm.

'I felt him shudder and collapse against me. After a few seconds he sort of shook 'imself, pulled my dress down and walked out. I heard 'im drive away. I collapsed on the sofa. Ben found me later; sound asleep with the groceries still in the car - the ice-cream and other cold stuff ruined. I had to tell 'im a story about feeling sick. He put me to bed with some water and a book."

Nikki couldn't concentrate on reading. Her thoughts were full of the stranger who had given her so much pleasure. Her imagination took her to the future, creating scenarios where she would see him in the street again, where they would steal an hour or two - slower this time.

Ben went to work early the next morning; there was a valuable horse foaling and he had to rush off and attend to the birth. Nikki was outside in the clear morning, enjoying the benign sunshine that would turn fierce later, loving the feel of her body, which had been feeling languorous since the afternoon before. She remembered having a smile on her face that morning, happy that she had a secret that was all hers. She felt lucky to have this thing - this precious memory that was hers alone.

She sensed a shift in the air before she saw the dust rising up the driveway. It was early for visitors. She had been filling the horse troughs, but turned off the tap and began walking toward the front of the house. For a minute she thought it might be the stranger returning and her heart began beating wildly, but as she walked out of the shadow of the house and onto the driveway, she saw her mother's car approaching. Considering it was only seven in the morning, and that her mother lived four hours away by car, Nikki knew that something major had happened.

She walked to the driver's door and pulled it open. "I started firing questions at me mum. What was wrong? Was it Dad? Was it bad news? Me mum just looked at me and said she needed a cuppa and a sit down. We went inside and I made the tea. Mum just started talkin' then, flat out, like, and taking things out of her handbag to show me."

It was a long story, and her mother took nearly an hour to tell it. It began when she met a boy and fell in love. He was handsome and strong, and he seduced her easily. He left her, a pregnant and tearful nineteen year old, as easily as he would shed a jacket.

There were no secrets in the outback, only shame for a girl who'd gotten herself 'in trouble'. Her parents acted swiftly. There was a farmer on a neighbouring property who'd lost his young wife in a mustering accident. During his short marriage he had been found to be infertile. He needed a wife and he wanted a child. She needed a husband. Down the aisle they went. All fixed.

"I was listenin' to her a bit, you know…well I wasn't really listenin'. She was droning on and on and I just wanted to be alone, like, to think about the day before. She'd come bustin' in, spoiling my happiness to tell me a stupid story about 'er and some bloke, and then the penny dropped,you know. I realised what she was tellin' me. Me dad wasn't me dad. Some other bloke was."

This certainly got Nikki's attention. She and her dad had been close all her life. She had a deep love and respect for him. Now, all of a sudden, he was not her father.

"So I asked her, like, why now? Why come an' tell me all this now? Why spoil me belief that I had the best dad in the world? Mum burst into tears and told me that people had seen 'im — my real father—in town the day before. The stories goin' 'round were that he had fallen on rough times and had shown up again like a bad penny. He'd been asking about her, me mum that is, but also about any child she might have 'ad. She was worried that he would try to talk to me and tell me the truth before she could."

The objects her mother had taken from the handbag

were lying face down on the kitchen table. There was a newspaper clipping and a photograph. Her mother nodded her head toward them, and Nikki turned the first one over. She sucked in her breath and reached hurriedly for the second one, hoping it would negate the first. In the clipping and the photograph, the face of the stranger from yesterday looked cheekily at her from a distance of twenty-five years.

"Me mum could tell straight away that something was wrong, and was at me and at me to tell her what it was. I just told her that I'd been sick the night before, and that Ben had put me to bed early, and that I wasn't quite right yet. She looked like she didn't believe me, so I called Ben's mobile, and me mum spoke to him, and he told her the story. She still looked at me funny-like though.

'I just wanted her to be gone so I could think this through without her talkin' to me all the time. Trying to make up for twenty-five years of lies, she was. Tryin' to explain and wanting me to see her side of it. I said I was okay, but that I felt sick and I had to go and lie down. She was going to stay to look after me, but I shooed her away."

Nikki was lost for words to try and explain the thoughts and feelings she experienced for the rest of that day. She couldn't do any chores or read anything. She just looked into the distance and ran it all though her mind, time and time again. The big question in her mind was whether or not he had known for certain that she was his daughter at the time they'd had sex. The thought that he did know chilled her to the bone.

Two weeks later she felt tenderness in her breasts. She checked the dates and found her period was three days late. As she stood there, looking at the dusty calendar, the one with horses on it that had been given to her by the flirty butcher, she found she couldn't hear the clocks ticking or the birds chirping. She couldn't feel the floor she was standing on. Her body, which had felt so alive and wonderful to her two weeks before, now felt dead and numb. It was now the enemy.

"I said to meself....I said...'Holy crap. I gotta get rid of this thing.'"

She looked at me with big, haunted eyes. "You're the only person I've told, you know? Do ya see why this 'ad to 'appen and quick, like? Me 'usbands a vet. He would 'ave known. Would 'ave looked at me and, like… just known. I can't tell 'im what I told you. I couldn't 'ave gone ahead and 'ad the bub. It was probably a monster."

She picked up the edge of the sheet and dabbed her eyes.

"It's not my fault you see." Her eyes were pleading.

"You do see that, don't cha?"

I wondered how Nikki's story would fit with the others. Then I wondered how all the stories would make a book. I knew my time for listening to and collecting stories was over, but I didn't have enough of them.

That's when the jolt of inspiration hit me. I would write about my journey here and include those stories. How exactly would I do it?

Just then I saw the very tip of the moon rising over the horizon. The staircase began forming and I held my breath in wonder. As my lunar friend rose higher, my thoughts of the book escalated as well. By the time the staircase had disappeared and the moon was higher in the sky, I was writing in my brain. I ran inside to where the soft light from a lamp fell across a small table, and began writing the words that have formed this book.

# CHAPTER SEVENTEEN

Christine bounced into my study, all blonde hair and pink cheeks. She smelled clean and gorgeous.

"Hey, honey-bunch. Whatcha up to?"

"Have a look." I turned the monitor for her to view.

"Wow that's amazing!" We both looked at the screen, split into four. Each view was of a different part of our townhouse as seen through the webcams I'd installed the previous day.

"I'll install a couple more later this week and also attach microphones to a couple of them."

"So, where can you view this from?"

"Anywhere in the world, as long as you have a PC and an internet connection."

"Amazing. You're so clever!" she said, ruffling my hair. "Hey, I've asked a couple of people over for dinner on Saturday night. We're not doing anything, are we?"

I fought my instinctive response and didn't let Chris see how unsettled I was at this news.

"Who are they?"

"He's Anthony and she's Sarah. They are husband and wife. They bought a car from me and, we got to know each other fairly well. They're friendly and caring people, really gorgeous. I just know you'll be very comfortable with them."

"What do they do?"

"Oh, he's a doctor of some sort. She's a musician with the Queensland Symphony Orchestra."

"Which section?"

"Um, strings, I think. She'll tell you herself on Saturday night. He wears the pants in the family and she seems to like it that way. I don't think they have any children."

"Okay. That all sounds fine."

"I might cook that duck dish I saw on that cooking show last week. I've got a few days to get it sorted."

She kept talking about catering while my concentration went back to working on the security system.

We had been robbed a few weeks earlier. Strangely, we were both at home, upstairs watching a DVD when it happened. They jumped a fence in the backyard and entered through an unlocked bedroom door downstairs.

They concentrated on our bedside tables, snatching jewellery and other items, while leaving muddy footprints on our pristine white carpet.

Chris was inconsolable when the theft was discovered. I tried to tell her that the stolen items were just 'objects' and that the important thing was that no one was attacked or hurt. For a few days she was nervy and kept checking that the doors were locked.

I decided to install the security system in an attempt to make her feel more secure in our home. Once this phase was finished, I would put sensors on the doors, and then have the whole system monitored by a security firm. I couldn't have Chris unsettled, because if she was then so was I.

She was talking about the wine for the dinner party, and then stopped. "Oh, sorry. I'll leave you in peace." She kissed me on the top of my head and bounced out of the room, happy in her plan-making.


Anthony and Sarah were just as Chris had described, friendly and sociable. They radiated warmth and goodwill, although Anthony could talk a bit forcefully at times.

Chris had done well with the catering. We had prawn

cocktails for an entrée, and then a duck dish that was tender and tasty. I didn't eat much of it; the richness was already making my stomach queasy, but I had some of the cheese platter afterwards.

The conversation had flowed pleasantly the whole time. I mostly let the three of them talk and just queried Sarah on her musical career. She played the violin for our state orchestra and had done so for two years.

I let the conversation flow around and over me. My mind was wandering to my study and things I was working on in there. My fingers were itching to hit some keys.

"Hey," said Chris looking at me. "Anthony has a new tablet and he's having problems with it. Perhaps you can give him some advice?" I felt a surge of adrenalin.

"Sure." I looked at Anthony. "Is it an Android?"

"Er, yes. Yes that's it. Android."

"Honeycomb?"

Three faces looked at me blankly.

"That's a version of Android. Like Windows XP or Windows 7."

"Ah, I see. I don't know."

"Well if you only just purchased it," he nodded, "then it's likely to be Honeycomb, although a couple are being released with IceCreamSandwich as we speak."

"Ah, I see. Okay..."

"What make and model is it?"

He told me, and I was able to confirm the version of the operating system. Then I asked what his problems were.

They were all mostly minor, but frustrating for him. He could fix them with a combination of adjusting the settings and downloading some apps to help the machine do what he wanted. I began telling him what to do.

Chris interrupted. "Perhaps you could write it down for Anthony, step-by-step? I think most of this is over his head."

That explained the look he had been giving me. I went and got a pen and pad and began writing, filling three sheets.

Anthony took the pieces of paper and pocketed them with a smile. "I'm lucky that I got talking to someone so knowledgeable. How long have you had yours?"

"Oh, I don't own one."

"Then how do you know so much?"

"Just from computing magazines. Also my phone runs Android."

"Yes," said Chris, "I buy Vogue and cooking magazines. Janine buys the ones about computers."

The topic of conversation was changed to cooking,

and I began fidgeting. The great thing about Chris was that she didn't mind if I excused myself and bolted to the study when I felt I had to. She asked if I wanted to top up my wine, but I shook my head and left the room.

As I slid into my computer chair I sighed with satisfaction. The first thing I did was write a couple of pages about Anthony and his wife to help me settle down. Then I opened the security software. While there were people in the house it was a perfect time to test the new microphones.

I went to camera one and could see Chris and our guests rising from the table. They picked up their glasses, and Chris took the bottle of wine before they moved out of sight. Soon they were visible on camera four, on the deck, sitting looking into the canopy of the neighbour's trees behind us.

I turned the microphone on and adjusted the volume. I made a few further adjustments and their voices became clear. They were discussing the view, and I wasn't taking any notice of what was being said. Sarah asked where the bathroom was and excused herself.

I was about to move to another zone when I heard Chris say, "Anthony, I'm afraid I had an ulterior motive for inviting the two of you tonight."

Anthony sat forward in his char. "Well, this is intriguing. Tell me more!"

She laughed. "Oh, nothing exciting, I can assure you. I found out what field you specialise in, and how well you're regarded. I believe you are a world expert."

"So you wanted me to come and meet Janine informally, *in situ* as it were?"

Even in the semi-darkness, through a web-cam, I could see Chris's shoulders slump. "I didn't realise it was that obvious."

"Not to the average person, I can assure you. Females are a lot harder to pick than males, but I've been working with a lot of females recently and have gotten pretty good at spotting them." He cleared his throat and sat straighter in the seat. "It's all in how the brain is wired. Women, you see, communicate using both hemispheres of the brain, whereas men only use one side. Women are also adept at imitating other women – taking cues from Alpha females on how to behave. These two factors combine to make life a lot easier for them."

I sat transfixed. They were talking about me and I had absolutely no idea what their words meant.

"What traits did you pick up first?"

"Oh, the sociability problems. That gave me my first

clue. Then what happened when you mentioned the tablet - that was clever of you, by the way. Her response was textbook for the condition. A real dump of data."

"Yes, that's what happens when you get her talking about technology."

"Then I looked at her clothing. All soft and loose. I'd bet they're natural fibres."

"Yes, all pure cotton, merino and silk."

"Does she have stomach or intestinal problems?"

"Oh, yes. Is that part of the condition? The meal we had will upset her later."

"Did you know that as many as 75% of people on the spectrum have those problems?"

I opened a browser and typed 'on the spectrum' into a search-engine window. Soon the results were pouring onto the page. I opened the first link and only then realised what they were talking about.

"Her usual diet is plain and bland to try and avoid problems. Often, if she is concentrating on a novel, or a computer problem, she will simply forget to eat."

"Does she have the fine motor skills problems?"

"Yes, just a bit clumsy."

"How about the problems with finding her way to places?"

Chris laughed. "Oh, yes. The GPS navigation system is a godsend for her."

"So she's never been tested?"

"For the syndrome? No and I'm certain she is totally unaware. The only reason I realised she might have it is that my mother's sister is very much like her. I'm very fond of this aunt, and when I told my mother that I'd met someone just like Aunt Lily, Mum questioned me and then told me about her sister's recent diagnosis."

"With women it often remains undiagnosed until one of its associated problems escalates. Depression, for instance."

"I don't think Janine has ever suffered from that."

"It is my belief that depression isn't a symptom of the syndrome. It often occurs as a result of problems the syndrome causes. That might be relationship or employment issues, for instance."

"Oh, okay. I can see that now. So Janine, who has never had employment problems and who is happy in our relationship, has no reason to suffer depression?"

"That's it. Has she been in other relationships?"

I began squirming in my seat. Being talked about, and in such intimate terms, didn't sit well with me. I noticed that one of the search results pointed to an online test for the syndrome. I clicked on the link to the website and began answering the questions.

"Yeah, married twice. Even has a son."

"How did she feel about being a mother?"

"It was the husband's idea. I don't think she was keen. She seemed to be okay as a parent, though."

"Yes, that's also a trait. They can make good but unconventional parents. They don't believe that normal gender roles apply to them."

"Should I suggest to her that she get tested?"

"Maybe, but hers is obviously a mild case. She's very high-functioning. I just don't see how it's causing any major issues at the moment."

I completed the test and clicked on the submit button. The average score out of 50 was 16.4. Any score above 32 meant that further testing was recommended. My score was 33.

"So you think we should just let sleeping dogs lie?"

"I can't see how being tested would benefit her at the present time. There's no cure, you see. All we can do is treat any problems that arise from it. I can't see that she needs treatment. Ah, here's Sarah back!"

I found another online test. This one had a lot more questions. I started filling them out, my fingers flying across the keyboard.

I heard Sarah's chair scraping across the deck and possums rustling in the bushes. Someone poured more wine in a glass. The conversation resumed, but it was dull. I completed the test and submitted the answers. The results came back quickly. I was probably on the spectrum.

I found a blog written by a woman who was recently diagnosed after years of misdiagnoses. This delay in finding the real reason for her issues resulted in addictions and law-breaking.

Another blogger wrote about daily problems she faced, and she sounded a lot like me. Another site listed the traits. Most applied to me with the exception of melt-downs and depression.

Looking back now I remember how I felt as I sat back in the chair and chewed the inside of my mouth. In one way it was a revelation. It explained so much. Now I could see there was a clearly defined template that could be fitted to my feelings and behaviour.

In another way it was disturbing. I needed to find out more. I read through more search results.

Not much later there was a knock on the door. Chris poked her head around. "They're leaving, do you want to come and say goodbye?"

I reduced the browser and followed her to the front door. Our guests said goodnight warmly and Anthony thanked me for my help with the tablet.

We closed the door behind them and smiled at each other. I helped Chris clean the kitchen, all the time waiting for her to raise the subject of my condition. She didn't say a word.

Days went by. I became an expert on Asperger's Syndrome while waiting for Chris to talk to me about it. Once I even raised the subject of Anthony, asking what field he specialised in, but she was vague in her response. I needed her to tell me what this meant, how it affected our relationship. I needed to know why she'd gone about it the way she had, so secretively, but I couldn't find the words to ask her.

That dinner party was held when the moon was waning, five days before the no-moon, the one when I left work early to go home and make love to my beautiful Christine, wanting to feel the magic of the moon's absence.

# CHAPTER EIGHTEEN

I picked up my pen and notebook on that night after witnessing the staircase to the moon, and began writing the words that have formed this story. In the past two weeks I have only stopped to sleep or to enter the pages into the word processor on my laptop. I wake late, write freehand, type for a few hours, have a brief swim, then come back and write freehand again until I fall asleep.

I am at my most creative in the late afternoon and into the night. Sometimes I write until three in the morning. When I type my work the next day, I often see an illegible scrawl where I have fallen asleep while still holding the pen.

This writing kept the darkness at bay although it still hovered just out of my range of sight. If I went to bed before I'd entered a state of total exhaustion, or before I'd had enough vodka, The Darkness came closer, trying to force my surrender. That's all in the past now, though. The darkness no longer sits at a distance, but I will tell you about that in a moment.

First I have to explain what I have done in relation to my novels and poems. A few days ago I developed a website and purchased a domain name. This also came with a website hosting package. I uploaded the web pages and then converted all my novels, short stories and poems to pdf format and uploaded them, linking each one to a corresponding item on the website. There is only one more piece of work to upload, this one, and I will finish it tonight.

I added tags to the site and also performed other search engine optimisation tasks. People looking for literary fiction, poetry and free e-books will find their way to my web pages.

There is a lawyer that works in the same firm who gives the Boss legal advice. I have met him several times and liked him. I have made contact and told him what I need. He will administer any enquires generated by the website that relate to publishing any of the work. His name appears as a contact. He will also act for me in other matters.

After I have uploaded this book, I will send an email to Anne, the editor I met in Daly Waters. She can be the first to read my work, and in the unlikely event she finds any that is marketable, can have first option of publishing it.

Yesterday I ticked off the last of the tasks on a long list. I knew I only had to finish this chapter and was delaying it until today, the no-moon day. I was sitting on the balcony, looking out to sea and found that the darkness had sat beside me and taken my hand, just like an old friend would. We sat there, like this, for an hour or so, companionably. Last night when I went to bed, I felt it spoon up against my back and this time it was welcome. It cupped my left breast with its right hand and we became one.

It was nowhere to be seen this morning but I could feel it in my body like a warm, heavy, oily weight. It talks to my brain, a constant stream of thoughts and ideas. This is what it has suggested to me:

*The no-moon is a time to resolve, to finish, to finalise, to bring those things to an end that appeared beyond resolution;*

*The reason I hadn't been able to visualise my life beyond the no-moon was because there is nothing beyond it;*

*Although I have struggled to find peace, it is at hand. I just have to reach out and grasp it.*

It then told me what to do. It was so obvious that I was amazed I hadn't thought of it myself.

Now I will email my sister - no - I'll hand write a letter

to her. It will be a long one in which I will try to explain the inexplicable.

I have made some weighty decisions today and there is one that will be the hardest to execute. Five people told me stories and let me enter their lives in an acutely personal way. In some cases the telling of the story was an act of bravery because the stories were so heart-wrenching.

I haven't been brave. The story of what happened on that last day in Brisbane has been locked away. The only way I've been able to make this journey, to go through the necessary actions, is by fighting the memory and pushing it away if it tried to surface.

Now, however, I will write my own story, telling of those few minutes that changed me so profoundly. I owe it to those other five people.

Then this book will be complete.

After that there will be only one more thing to do.

At midnight I will walk down to the beach and then walk across the flats until I enter the water. I'll wade out until it reaches my waist. Then I will begin swimming.

I will swim breast-stroke so I can see my destination with every smooth cycle of movement. I will be swimming towards the place where the moon should be. I will swim towards the absence of the moon, the darkness that is the twin of the darkness inside of me. When my darkness unites with the darkness of the absence, I will be at peace.

I will swim toward the void, which is caused by the no-moon, in order to mate it with my own void, that which was caused by the loss of Christine. My soul is now black and it will merge with the blackness of the place where the moon should be.

I will arrive at this place with a sigh of surrender. My soul will fly from me to this place of darkness, free and without pain. Oh, to be rid of the pain!

When you search the night skies for the moon and find it isn't there, think of me. Know that the sky isn't empty, for I will be there. I will live in the place of the no-moon for eternity.

# JANINE'S STORY

I woke that morning with a smile on my face and wondered about it. A happy dream? An exceptionally good night's sleep? I was lying on my side with my arm flung across the softness of Chris's waist. There was a slippery coating of perspiration where our skin had been touching. Chris was snoring softly as she always did after a big drinking session, this time with the other salespeople to celebrate a record month.

I turned on to my back and slid over to the cooler side of the bed. I could see the first rays of sun creeping in around the edges of the curtains. Soon the birds began cheeping and I knew it was one of those stunning September mornings. I had to get out into it.

I felt light, both physically and mentally, and it was a beautiful sensation. I felt joy in the thud of my feet on the footpath, and again in the transition from cement to grass when I got to the oval. The soft turf, still dewy, was a delight.

As I ran back into the house I was throbbing with energy. I felt powerful and fully sexually charged. My brain was clear and my vision sharp. I quickly prepared for work and wrote Chris a note, signing it with a smiley face.

Chris was the lucky member of the sales team; her rostered day off just happened to fall on the day following the celebrations. I figured the rest of the sales department would be fairly useless and wondered about the condition of the Boss, who had hosted the event.

I could hear his voice from downstairs, barking instructions with a tone of irritability. I took a deep breath and climbed the stairs, readying myself for an onslaught.

"Ah, Janine. Thank God you're here at last!"

I looked at my watch in puzzlement. I was early.

"Look, I want to clean all this shit off my desk before golf. Those other monkeys never understand what I want. Let's get to it."

He started flinging paperwork at me while issuing instructions that were low on detail and high on bad language. I followed him around with a notebook, writing furiously as his demands landed around me like incendiary devices.

Even this couldn't kill my mood. I fell into the rhythm and answered his questions without hesitation. I was on fire.

Finally he collapsed into his chair, blowing his cheeks out. "That just about does it. Hey, could you run me to Royal Queensland? I'm going to stay for a few drinks after the round."

He took the driver's seat as usual, and I could feel him calming down the further we got from the dealership.

"So, what's up for the weekend?" he said.

I felt like a rabbit caught in the headlamps. He and I didn't often talk about personal matters, especially mine.

"Well, tomorrow afternoon I'm flying to Sydney to see that play with Cate Blanchett in it and then flying back on Sunday."

"How in the hell did you get tickets for that?"

"Oh, just good timing, really."

"Bloody hell. The wife wanted to see it but missed out. She's been moaning about it. I should have put you in charge of making sure we got tickets. Who are you going with?"

"Just Chris from Sales. We'll leave as soon as she knocks off."

"You two seem to be pretty good mates. I hear you're sharing an apartment. How do you find that?"

I framed my answer carefully. "Oh, good. It suits both

of us well. She's a bit messy but we rub along okay."

"Good, good. No chance of going back to David then?"

I laughed at the absurdity of the idea. "A definite no. He's got someone else, and she's good for him, and I'm better off where I am."

He nodded thoughtfully. "So you're happy then?"

I wondered how much he knew about Chris and I. Was it an open secret?

"Yes thanks. I'm great."

"Listen, I was a bit rough on you this morning. Sorry about that."

I began protesting.

"No, I mean it. You're a good gal and I don't want you to think I don't appreciate you. Why don't you take the rest of the day off?"

For a moment I thought about the remainder of work on my desk, but I knew there wasn't anything urgent.

I accepted his offer gratefully and felt a gentle smile come to my face as I watched him struggle to unload his clubs from the back of the car and waddle off toward the clubhouse, waving his hand in a kind of salute. He was one of the good guys.

I didn't spend long back at work, just long enough to

change cars and grab the laptop. I said a cheery goodbye to the receptionist, telling her I'd be working from home for the afternoon. Her response was a jealous scowl.

Knocking off work early added to my amazing feeling of lightness. I thought about surprising Chris; there was even a chance she'd still be in bed, and that led me to thinking about an afternoon of lovemaking. I took a detour to buy her favourite French champagne from an upmarket wine shop in The Valley.

As I turned into our street a realisation dawned on me. I stopped the car and tapped the app shortcut on my mobile. The picture of the dark moon flashed onto the screen with "0% of Full" underneath. My smile grew broader. Wow, what timing!

The garage door rose silently, and I was glad to see Chris' car still parked there. I backed mine in next to it and crept into the kitchen, where I grabbed two champagne glasses. I was almost giggling as I crept down the stairs, careful not to stand on those I knew creaked.

I was nearly to the bottom when I heard an awful sound. It was Chris and she sounded as though she was in agony. I took the last two steps quickly and ran into the bedroom.

She was being attacked. There was a man on top of

her and he had a rope around her neck. She was writhing and moaning, flinging her whole body from side to side.

The adrenaline flooded my body like water from a burst dam. I felt it hit my heart and my brain. My thoughts took on a cold, hard clarity. I dropped the bottle and glasses, and ran to the bed, screaming, "Leave her alone, you bastard! I'm going to call the police!"

I gave him a massive push that was driven by my fear and anger. It was so powerful that it flung him sideways off the bed. I picked the champagne bottle up by the neck, testing the weight in my other hand. I was ready.

The attacker lifted his head above the other side of the bed and I saw that it was Michael. Michael? I screamed, "What in the hell are you doing? Why would you hurt Chris? What has she ever done to you?"

I walked toward Chris to see if she was okay. She was naked. The rope was still around her neck and she was reaching to remove it. I noticed absently that the rope was unusual; it was soft looking with tassels at each end. She sat up, her face as pale as the sheet she was drawing up around herself.

"Honey, Janine. It's all okay. He wasn't trying to hurt me."

I looked from one to the other and saw, as Michael

stood, that he too was naked, a fact that hadn't registered in my brain until then.

"It's just a sex thing. I wanted to try it. More powerful orgasms, they say. I asked him to do it to me."

Michael's penis was shiny and slippery looking. I realised he must have been inside Chris when I came into the room.

The cold clarity was deserting me, a terrible confusion taking its place. I knew it wouldn't be long before I imploded.

"Michael," I said, "Get out of here now. Go straight to your father's. Don't call me. If you do I'll tell him and Jodie what you just did."

Pale with shock, he covered his groin with his big hands and ran out of the room.

I looked at Christine. She held her arms out to me, beseechingly. There was something in her face I couldn't read, a look I'd never seen there before. Then I felt it in the air. Fear. Fear? She knew I wasn't a violent person, so she didn't have to worry about her safety. What was she afraid of?

Snapshots of our life together ran through my brain like a movie in fast-motion: all the presents I bought for her, the holidays, her expensive gym membership, facials, massages, clothes, restaurants. She never seemed to have money of her own and I paid for almost everything. Was that what she was afraid of, that she'd blown it all?

I only had seconds left. After that I'd be incapable of rational thought.

"In my bed, with my son. That's a pretty low act."

She lowered her head and I could see her bottom lip begin to tremble.

"I'm going now. I have to get out of here. I don't know when I'll be back."

She looked up, her pupils growing huge.

"I ask only one thing of you. Don't say anything now and don't call me or try to contact me in any way. As long as you don't, you can stay here and use the money in the slush fund. Contact me and all this," I waved my arms around the room, "will disappear."

She chewed her lip and remained silent.

I looked at her and waited, hearing my heart thudding in my chest. I waited for her to ignore my instructions, waited for her to fold me in her arms and explain it all away, tell me it's all okay like she always did. I waited for her to prove that she cared for me more than she cared about her own comfort and security. She lowered her eyes to the sheets, her lips pressed tightly together.

A few more seconds ticked by. I turned and ran out of the room and up the stairs. By the time I reached the car I was shaking uncontrollably. I sat in the driver's seat with my head on the steering wheel chanting, "Come to me. Come to me. Come to me." My voice was breaking. I fumbled and dropped the keys, finally getting them into the ignition.

At last, the engine fired and I stamped on the accelerator and shot out of the garage.

# EPILOGUE

I first met Janine on a lonely stretch of road between Tenant Creek and Daly Waters, in the outback of the Northern Territory in Australia.

She had suffered the indignity of a flat tyre and we stopped to assist.

We met up again in Daly Waters, and I found her fascinating. This was a woman totally unconscious of her beauty and the wealth of her intellect. She seemed to move through the world hesitantly: shyly and a bit sadly. Her eyes were expressive, but I had trouble seeing what was behind them. The shutters would come down and she would look away.

We ended up talking well into the night. Without knowing what I did for a living, she told me about the book she was writing. I queried her about any previous work and found out she had a massive collection that had never been read by anyone but herself.

When she found out I was an editor for a major

publishing house, she became embarrassed and withdrawn. I gently coaxed her out of this state and asked to see her work.

There must be many writers like her in the world, those driven to write because they must. They don't think about profit or fame, but pour their stories onto pages and hide them away. I believe these are the people who find life hard and confusing. History is full of them.

Sadly Janine took her own life, in the manner she described, on the night she planned. Fortunately, however, she also sent me a link to her website, which contained that body of great work. I persuaded the publishing company I work for to buy the entire collection, and it has since closed the website down.

Her manuscripts, though only first drafts, were in excellent shape. I have allowed only minor editing - spelling, punctuation and some minor grammar. This way the reader will experience the excellence of Janine's writing without the distraction of small errors.

I hope they give you as much pleasure as they did me.


Anne Fuller.

## ACKNOWLEDGMENTS

Many people are generous with their own time in all stages of getting my novels to print. To these people I will be eternally grateful.

## ABOUT THE AUTHOR

Brenda Cheers is a writer of both short and long fiction.

She lives in Brisbane, Australia with her partner and two daughters.

See more at:  brendacheersbooks.com  .